# A Man Who ~~Fut~~

## W.J.Lane

Copyright © 2012 Author Name

All rights reserved.

ISBN: 150595133X
ISBN-13: 978-1505951332

### DEDICATION

To Mother, To Brother

This is a work of fiction. Names, characters, businesses, places, events and incidents are either the products of the author's imagination or used in a fictitious manner. Any resemblance to actual persons, living or dead, or actual events is purely coincidental.

First Publishes December 2014

© 2014 W.J.Lane

www.wjlane.com

## Prologue

So I'm momentarily knocked out and wake up with a gun in my mouth. Phil is knelt on my chest - his manic eyes are inches from my face, his overweight frame crushing my lungs and slowly seeping the life from me. He is snarling words at me that I can barely understand as my ears are ringing wildly. A liquid runs down the back of my right leg and I assume it's from the gunshot wound and not my bladder, as he pins me to the concrete floor.

Over his shoulder, I see a women fleeing from the back of the van, its destructive cargo still lying in wait. Off to my right I see the detonator in pieces. Phil, now recognising both these occurrences, is further enraged and swings his elbow across the side of my face.

I can taste all of the following things; blood, sweat, saliva, metal, powder, and oil.

"WHY DID YOU HAVE TO GET INVOLVED?", Phil scream's at me whilst taking a couple more swipes with his elbow, each one giving me a brief window for breath as he has to remove the gun from my mouth to do so. Each one chipping a tooth or two as he shoves the barrel back down my throat.

I swallow several chunks of enamel during these blows. The barrel of the gun tastes smooth and polished against my tongue, and I can feel tiny indentations and markings along the surface with it. My ears have been pierced by the gunshots and I can now feel blood trickling down the side of my face.

I am going to die - this much is certain. The damage is already done and I am strangely content knowing this, the bile and rage spewing forth from my attacker is virtually irrelevant.

I know all these things at this point; that this will be my last day on earth; that Alice will be safe; that it is hard to breath with a gun in your mouth; that having a 17 stone man pressing on your chest is uncomfortable; that Alice will take care of Dex for me; that I will make the news.

Phil pulls the gun out of my mouth, and his tears shower my face as he strikes me across the side of the head with its butt. I black out again and must be seconds from death because various things flash before my eyes. I see myself wetting the bed as a kid, calling for a mother who doesn't appear. I see my dad drinking heavily on my birthday whilst my mother lambastes him for it. Later I see dad disappear forever after him and mum had a huge row. I see myself running away from home as a teenager and sleeping on various friends' floors, eventually returning to the family home months later, just in time to watch my mother slowly getting ill and then die in front of me. I see myself losing my virginity to a hooker at 17 - spending £60 for the pleasure. I see flashbacks of my various careers including roadie, musician, writer, magician, window cleaner, electrician, painter and decorator and psychic. I see Dex licking my face to wake me up from a hideous hangover, and Alice snuggling up to me in the back of the cinema. I see my shitty flat complete with rising damp and Dex's various stains. I see my crappy life fading into nothing and it doesn't matter anymore.

    I just see Alice happy and it's all I need.

    I see her smile and I am ready for death.

    I close my eyes because I'm ready for death.

    I hear a gunshot and am ready for death.

# Chapter 1

So this is what my job entails - sitting opposite strangers, seeing the truth, but telling them lies. Right now we have a young and attractive brunette named Jean. She's fresh faced and full of the optimism of youth, bright and rosy skinned with a flawless complexion; perfect housewife material no doubt.

She sits opposite me and watches eagerly as I fiddle around with some props. Often I use various dice, tarot cards, precious stones and even when I'm feeling the showman, a crystal ball. I use these things to flesh out the sitting, give it a little drama and make them feel I'm at least making some effort. People feel short changed if I make predictions without actually waving anything around or displaying a prop of some kind. They want a show for their £15.

All I really need to see your future is a personal possession of some kind and a brief moment of focus. See unlike every other fairground psychic, fortune teller, mystic, fraudster etc; I can actually see the future.

Not a watered down, vague bullshit version of the future - the actual stone cold future. I CAN see your future, given a trinket; I WILL see visions of your future flash before my eyes. Brief snippets of events and glimpses of things to come, not cliché nonsense like the lottery numbers this weekend or the winner of the Grand National, exact moments in your life to come.

It is a gift and sometimes a curse - but right now a career.

So I gaze at the sprawled dice like they mean something. They are 12 sided and adorned with tiny little symbols that could mean anything and everything, depending on what mood I'm in. I sigh and make intriguing noises whilst waving a quizzical hand above the die. I hold a finger to my temple, gaze across at Jean intently and request the locket dangling around her neck. Intrigued, she hands it over and I clasp it in my right hand tightly whilst focusing hard.

This is what I see of Jean's future.

She marries her current boyfriend - the one she loves intensely - the one she came in here to hear good things about. She's dressed in white and walking down the aisle, its picture perfect and her groom is every bit the stud such and attractive women deserves. She's a princess for the day and everyone is doting over the happy couple. They go to Barbados and she gets knocked up during the first few days of their honeymoon.

Life is perfect for a while.

Then I see her crying alone in front of the TV as Mr Stud calls her late again from the 'office'. He's fucking someone else, because she is heavily pregnant and hasn't been interested in sex for a while. Also he is not the perfect man she thinks he is.

I see her crying a lot and having screaming rows with him every time he rolls in at 11pm or 3am. I see her pleading with him to love her better and then I see her begging him not to leave. I see her, on her knees, sprawled over his suitcase in the hallway as he gets his keys and walks out on his heavily pregnant wife. I see that "he is a grade A scumbag and your better off without him," as her mother consoles her repeatedly later.

Still focusing and clutching her gold locket, I see her ascending the stairs one evening drunk, alone, and scared that she will have to give birth any day now without her husband. I see her stumble on stair no.9 and clutch hopelessly at the banister. I see her stuffed bunny slippers give way out on the edge of the stairs.

I see her tumble backwards down the staircase.

I see blood and tears.

I see an ambulance and I see her inconsolable in a hospital bed. Her mother is there and so is Mr. Perfect. It was his baby too and although his actions led to this, he is distraught at the turn of events.

I skip several years here and then I see her in a small flat, still alone but now divorced. I see her watching the soaps after an arduous day at her 9-5 admin job. I see her dreams broken and her outlook bleak. She has put on significant amounts of weight in the interim years and now has only a small housedog for companionship.

I see a broken, unattractive and overweight woman, living out her years in relative solitude after Mr. Perfect scared her off serious commitment forever. I see a tattoo of the name Brady on her wrist - her chosen name for the lost child. Dreams are unrealised and her life plays out unfulfilled and unhappy. The outlook is bleak as I place the locket down carefully, trying to catch my breath.

This is where the moral conundrum of my gift comes into play. I could tell her everything? It will happen and it is her future; I could tell her to leave him, tell her what he will do to her, tell her that she should strike out into the world whilst she is young and full of opportunity. Don't get married at 25, don't have kids for another 10 years and don't wear ridiculous slippers whilst heavily pregnant.

I could tell her all of these things and more, I could try to change her life and her path, but I don't and I never do.

See people don't really want to hear the future - they want to be fed a vision of what they perceive the future will be. I've come to learn the following after doing this for a lifetime - people believe that there future will always be a lot better than current evidence seems to suggest.

Mr. Perfect has always stayed out late and played around. She knows this deep down, but seems to think marriage will change him. People believe the future will be everything they dream of; that they will have more money than they currently possess; that they will be much happier than they currently are; that life will be more satisfying than it currently is; that the sex will be better than ever.

People think the future holds all the answers and I know it doesn't.

So I just never tell them. Instead I look into the future for bright spots and try to pick these out. I tell her she will have the dream wedding and will conceive a child with the man of her dreams. I tell her the name Brady will forever be important to her. I tell her that her mother will be a rock on which to lean on for the rest of her life.

I tell her all these things and her face lights up. I feel like I've done the right thing, I feel like this is another happy customer, I feel like she is invigorated and enthused about the future when she leaves the reading. I feel like I've done a good job, but I also feel sick.

Sick to my stomach that this sweet innocent young thing, who just wants love and commitment - will be let down so badly by someone she loves so much, that fate has dealt her a cruel blow already. My gift makes me sick at the things I can't un-see, the horrors I've seen in people's futures, the endless breakdowns, traumas and chaos, that runs through a lifetime. These are the types of things I see everyday.

Could I tell people and give them a chance to change things? Maybe?

Would they believe me? No of course not.

Would Jean have listened to the friendly psychic if I told her to leave her Mr. Perfect? Would she have listened to me if I told her he is a serial cheat? Would she have wanted to hear about her depressing admin career?

The answers to all of these questions is no.

People don't want me to shatter their hopes and their dreams, so I don't. Jean leaves happy and optimistic. The future is bleak for her, for the majority of us, but she doesn't know that and that makes life easier for her to live.

When I first started doing this job I used to struggle to sleep at night, now I've just seen it all before.

# Chapter 2

It's later in the day now and I've just finished the short lunch break. That's if you can call a can of energy drink, an apple, and a healthy dose of futility a lunch? In this line of work, lunch breaks consists of a hanging 'back in 10' sign, a trip to the toilet and a small stroll around the fair.

Today the site is bustling with the kind of half term holiday masses that make all us traders and carnies excited. Everywhere, eager and happy punters are throwing their money at the plethora of attractions that litter the site. Everywhere small children are pestering their parents into winning them a giant stuffed banana. Groups of teenagers are queuing for rides that they think will make them more attractive to the opposite sex. All around people are having fun whilst I barely have time to evacuate my bowels.

The busier the fair the shorter the lunch breaks, and I speed across the site to the tiny portaloo's, devour an apple and return back to my van just in time to see an old dude stroking Dex heartily outside my van, awaiting my return.

He's a dear old dude, at least 70-80 in years, and wearing

the kind of high wasted shorts, sandal and socks combo, that only truly content old gentlemen can get away with. I can tell he's from a different generation, a different world, because he tips his hat towards me and greets me with an extremely polite, "Good day, kind sir, may I have reading please?" The kind of greeting that doesn't exist in the post war generations, the kind of excessive politeness that makes the rest of us slightly uncomfortable and uneasy in the modern world.

   I welcome him up the small staircase and into the van as we make small talk about the weather, and discuss how busy trade has been for me over the week. In fact he is so polite that he removes his flat cap and places it on his lap, as he takes his seat across from me.

   I do my thing and wave around some tarot cards, glancing at the Death, the Fool and the Justice cards in front of me like they are important. Then I ask for his hat and tell him I need it to gain an accurate reading. He hands it over without fuss and I glance at his cold, thin, pale hand as he does so - noticing the almost transparent skin and the thick blue vein trails that hide underneath.

   I realise this man is old, very old, the type of old that

makes you want to ask a million questions about how good/bad life used to be, about how people used to survive without the internet? Without on demand TV and instant gratification? About how men used to treat women with respect before the endless well of internet porn sprung forth and made us all just want to abuse them. This is the kind of man I wish to grow into; the kind I wished my father might be right now, if I knew anything about him. This is the kind of man that waits silently and patiently as I gaze across at his wispy hair and his haggard skin, the kind with endless patience and respect - the type that are in ever shorter supply.

I snap out of it and return to my reading where I see a lot more depressing stuff. I see this gent returning home to his empty bungalow. He sits in his chair and watches the cricket. Beside him sits an empty chair and a side table with a pair of knitting needles perched contently atop. Behind these needles sit a small ornate picture frame containing a black and white picture of an attractive young lady.

I see our gent gaze across at it longingly as the game breaks for tea. It's his long lost, but not forgotten, wife. A picture of her in her prime when their courting began. I see him shed a small tear and eventually fall asleep in his chair before the game resumes.

Flash to our gent strolling serenely along a seafront, hands clasped behind his back as he strolls slowly, but surely. He's happy but alone, content but wounded. I see in his eyes the pain and the loss of his soul mate, I see in his eyes the loneliness of old age as life leaves him behind and his bones start to grow weary. I see him chat to random strangers on the pier about nonsense just to have someone to talk too. He rides the bus home and bores a younger man next to him the entire time with tales of a different era.

I see him fall asleep in front of the TV once again as he can no longer bear to sleep in their marital bed. I see a flurry of visions of this man living his life out alone and forgotten, a man waiting for death and having nobody to share it with. A man forgotten.

Flash to his funeral, attended by only long lost friends and virtual strangers, as this man seemingly had no children and had outlived his siblings.

Then I'm back in the room suddenly, sat opposite this kind and warm old guy, as he sits and waits for me to tell him his future will be great. He's expecting to hear how his life won't be a trail of lonely walks and silent nights. He wants me to tell him that he's not going to be heartbroken and isolated until his death. He's not expecting to hear wild success stories and bright futures - just that he might have someone to talk to for the next few years.

   I stare across at him and tell him that I see great happiness and comfort in his future. That his remaining years will be full of unexpected adventure and pleasure and that the hard work he has put in during his lifetime will finally pay off. I tell him that companionship is due to come to him, and that his wounds will heal with time.

   I tell him all this and I feel like shit.

   I tell him all this and can barely look him in the eye as he deposits a tip on my table and wishes me a good day as he leaves. I tell him all this and feel guilty enough to take another break and walk around the fair with him and Dex for a while, making small talk with him and trying to assuage my guilt. Trying to feel like being his mate for 10 minutes might help in some way.

   He is a lonely old gent and he will stay this way, but I can't tell him that. Instead I just lie to him because that's how this works.

   I see the future but it's never bright enough to pass on.

I see the future and most of the time I wish I didn't.

## Chapter 3

The Great Psy Paxely is now done for the day - enough dolling out faint hope to random strangers. The die go away, the cards are packed up, the candles extinguished and the gypsy caravan locked up.

This is all for show of course - my real name is Bill but that's nowhere near exciting enough for a psychic. I have no gypsy past either so there's no genuine need for the trailer, just window dressing and just as pointless as the various reading props are. It's all part of the show, part of the experience and you have to look the part to be convincing.

Such pomp and fakery are ironic really, especially as I can actually predict these people's futures. Doing this over the years, I've come across many fortune tellers and mystics, all of them utterly convinced they are harbingers of things to come, all of them pertaining to have long and rich histories and explanations for their incredible 'gifts'. Everyone seems to have some superhero origin story that explains where there incredible mystical skills originated. How these gifts were inherited during some exotic accident or near death experience etc.

Obviously it's all a load of nonsense. There is no exotic tale to explain this, no grandiose explanation needed, I CAN see the future! Full stop.

I didn't get hit by some radioactive material, have a near death experience or get contacted by the dead, I didn't acquire my skills after spending some time up in the mountains with Buddhist monks and I wasn't touched by the lord. I don't need this kind of nonsense because I'm the real deal.

How do I know I'm the real deal? I know this because I was born with it and I've lived with it for 30+ years. I've had visions of people being hit by cars days before the actual events; I've seen a guy spiral into debt, lose his home and end up on the streets, months before I passed him in the flesh, begging for change.

There was the punter whom I foresaw getting steaming drunk the night before a flight to the US, only for him to sleep in and miss his flight. Very stupid and irresponsible until I saw that plane crash into one of those twin towers. The future duly played out and I saw him back at the fair a few years later, unchanged by his near death brush.

I've had a few visions of people posing with lottery

cheques; those giant oversized ones with lots of zeros on. Fate rewarding them for spending £2 at the newsagents. Those are rare happy endings, but I've got countless depressing tales of people for whom tragedy struck, of lives that were indefinitely changed by some cruel twist of fate.

I regularly get customers return who have been awestruck by the accuracy of my readings, word of mouth spreads and my customer base grows. Sometimes people come for a second opinion - some charlatan has told them that they'll get that promotion or that the investments they have made are sound and smart, and that they will live to a healthy, happy old age etc. Of course I'll get premonitions that contradict whatever they've been fed, but then I'll back them up anyway.

'I too can see great success in your career in the coming month',

'I see a peaceful and content old couple living out there days happily in a luxurious bungalow', 'I can see great happiness in your future due to the shrewd financial moves you have been undertaking', blah, blah, blah.

I spend 90% of my time lying to people because I don't want to destroy their dreams - I don't want to destroy the hope and optimism that is their lifeblood. The other 10% of my time is spent giving subtle hints about what is too come in these peoples futures; all in some vague hope that what I say might just make some kind of difference.

Does that make me a bad person? No it's the constant, excessive, drinking that does that.

So away goes the paraphernalia for another day. Out go the candles, away goes the table and chairs, the shabby chic curtains are drawn and generator disabled. Cash is counted, totalled and bundled into the pocket of my trench coat as the early hours start to encroach. I step out through the small arched door, ducking slightly as I go, and take in the calm, quite night around me. Tired traders are rushing around locking up for the evening and shutting up shop. Blaring music is extinguished and excessive bulbs are killed. The cold, dark night, will slowly reclaim the site as I lock up gypsy caravan and descend down the stairs.

Dex, my faithful companion, waits for me at the bottom of the staircase. He sits out here as I work, soaking up the atmosphere of the fair and enticing custom. No one can resist a dog and I'm pretty sure he does more in terms of advertising and awareness than my crappy sandwich board does.

Dex keeps me sane, keeps me grounded and keeps me happy. There are also two things you should know about my faithful canine companion from the outset: 1 - I rescued him from an abusive owner after some fairly horrific vision and, 2 - he can predict cancer and can communicate this to me.

These are both stories for another day.

For now the day is done and another bottle beckons, so I unsheathe Dex and start our trek back to the van. I often leave a day's work down beat and depressed, and due to this I've developed something of an alcohol dependency. Heavy lies this particular crown, and after a day's worth of tragic visions I do tend to seek solace in the arms of Mr. Jack and Mr. Daniel. About 35 years I've been able to see the future - 30 of these I've been depressed - 5 of these I've been an alcoholic.

# Chapter 4

Post work I do one of two things. Either I go home to my cramped flat above the local chip shop with Dex and watch some old school horror films, I have a particular fondness for the early works of Dario Argento. Or Ill drink until the early hours at the local boozer. Not social drinking you understand. I have no friends. No, the type of drinking that tells people you have a problem. The type of drinking they warn you about on pamphlets and they ask you about when you attend AA.

*Do you often drink alone and to excess?* Yes.

*Has your drinking caused you trouble in the past?*

Every day!

*Have you ever decided to stop drinking but only lasted a couple of days?*

Yes Of course.

*Have you missed days at work because of your drinking?*

Yes normally weeks.

*Do you ever experience 'blackouts'?*

More often than not!

Understand that I've been to AA, often and repeatedly.

I've had, and been, a sponsor. But you know what - didn't work, it's never really worked for me. Just other people with a similar problem whining about how terrible life is, complaining like it's going to change something. So boring was it that it used to drive me to drink!

I've come to realise over time that life is terrible and that hanging around complaining about it won't make any difference. Alcohol offers an escape, one I haven't been able to find anywhere else, so I just keep on drinking. I drink to escape. Yes I'm an alcoholic, but without it I'd probably have killed myself by now.

So life goes on and tonight I end up at home with Dex watching the Re-Animator for the 19th time. It's a classic horror about a university professor who is brought back to life by a colleague, kind of like Frankenstein but with more blood and extreme gore.

I'm tired and I slump in front of the TV on my dirty couch, sloughing my trench coat and boots into a rough pile inside the door as I do so. Below me I can hear the chip shop closing up shop for the night.

When I bought this place the estate agent used words like cosy, homely, compact, and investment opportunity, to try and persuade me. Truth is, it's in a good location for the fair and being situated above a chip shop made it too cheap to resist.

It is indeed a compact 1 bed flat with a kitchen/lounge room, small bathroom and tiny entrance hallway. It holds me, Dex, and my minimalist lifestyle competently. Sure the plain, tired décor, could do with some updating and my second hand furniture should probably be replaced, but it serves me well.

I have a decent sized living area with a moderately large TV, a huge stack of DVD'S, and enough windows to let in the outside world - so I'm just about content.

I have 4 beers by my right side and an Alsatian to my left. It's late and the silver moonlight fills the room along with the glow of the TV. Despite the movie playing I have muted the sound and am only half interested in the images being displayed.

Currently a man is injecting himself with a strange liquid to fight off fatigue.

I like to sit here after a day's work, a day's worth of visions, a day's worth of lies, and contemplate what I've been through. These are just some of the things I told people today; the future holds much promise for you siblings and you; you're vices and flaws are yours to overcome; your charity work will be rewarded with much prosperity in years to come; you will achieve the financial independence you crave; the lump that concerns you will turn out to be nothing. I pretty much tell people what they want to hear and can often find myself getting into much more detail than I really should.

Onscreen a man is talking to a severed human head which he has in a tray on his desk, the head is talking back.

I sink another beer and listen to the hubbub outside. My flat fronts onto a main road and even at this time of night/morning, the world is still stirring.

I like to listen to the world outside and imagine the kind of days these people have had. How much fun the shift in the chipper was today, how much trouble the drunk stumbling home from the pub is going to be in later, how bad are the parents of the young louts, currently skulking the alleyways behind my building?

Everyone is bored and just trying to find something to do to pass the time, to numb the pain. Some people take drugs, some vandalize local property and indulge in anti-social behaviour, and some people pretend a life serving pie and chips is what they have always dreamed of. I like to pass the time drinking alone with my dog.

Onscreen the severed head is now being held aloft by its former body whilst it reasons with a scientist.

# Chapter 5

So because I want you to like me, this is the story of how I came to live with an adult Alsatian with cancer predicting abilities.

It was a few years ago now that I welcomed into a reading, a respectable looking man. Mid 30's and dressed in s smart/casual jeans and polo shirt combo. He was well groomed and doused liberally in aftershave. It was immediately obvious that he was on some kind of date at the fair that evening, very keen to impress whoever his companion may have been. A faint ring around his wedding finger suggested a recent divorce or separation, and a guy firmly on the rebound.

We sat down for the reading and I dealt some tarot cards, and looked at them meaningfully for a minute or so. I like to let the tension built for dramatic effect.

Then I asked for his watch. A cheap and tacky silver plated thing with a flimsy clasp and noisy strap, he passed it over with more trepidation than you would expect for such a request. Looking at me as if I was about to fleece him for it.

The visions soon came.

I saw our mate, think his name was Greg but can't really remember, getting on like a house on fire with his date. I saw them loving the Ferris wheel, the Waltzers, the bumper cars, I saw him win her an elephant from one of those claw grabber machines. The first date was a roaring success.

I saw him go home that night to Dex and bestow great affection upon him. This was a broken man, damaged by his separation and this woman had breathed fresh life into him, he was excited and Dex lapped up his attention lovingly.

Cut to a few months later and Dex is in this guy's kitchen in the dark. It's late at night and he's howling for his owner. Evidently he has been left for a while unattended and alone. Greg was out with his women until the early hours that night.

A few more months down the line and poor old Dex is outside in the back garden; a small tarmac courtyard with little or no greenery or entertainment for him. He sits sulking in the corner of this concrete prison as the rain begins to fall. He has been given only a stack of cardboard for a bed and no shelter. He cowers from the rain and the cold as the night falls and our mate Greg is getting it on upstairs with his women.

Flash forward a year or so and I see Dex back in the kitchen of this house. A small gully kitchen fit enough for two or three adults to fit in at the most. He's been locked in there for days. A large bag of food cut open and left spilled in one corner, a half filled bucket of water left in the other corner. Faeces and urine carpet the floor and poor old Dex is covered in his own waste as he paces his prison, depressed and scared.

He has been abandoned and left to his own devices whilst Gregory swans of to Sharmal Sheik for the week with his women.

Cut to another year or so down the line and I see Dex out on the streets - wandering aimlessly, heartbroken, afraid and alone, along the dark and threatening streets.

Evidently, Greg's new woman doesn't like dogs and can't possibly move in with him whilst 'that' dog is still living there. Cue our mate tossing his best friend, his loyal companion and his confident during some troubled times, out on the street to fend for himself.

A dog is for life not just until you find another woman whom can't stand canines Greg!

Flash forward to Dex sleeping in a dingy alleyway, losing excessive weight and eventually coming to a sticky end courtesy of a HGV. The poor dog was so malnourished, ill and generally depressed, that he didn't notice he had wandered onto a dual carriageway. Later our mate Greg is charged with neglect and abuse by the authorities.

Now I'm not a violent man, far from it. I've not really got the frame or pain threshold for violence; more of a bitter, snide and sarcastic type as opposed to fisticuffs, but for a minute, a split second after the visions faded, I wanted to grab old Gregory by the lapels and throw him face first out of the caravan doors. Let his date see her new man with a face full of dirt and a black eye or two.

Obviously I didn't do this, physical abuse not good for business, instead I fed him some nonsense that I can no longer remember and sent him on his way.

I drank heavily that night and blacked out.

The coming days I found myself racked with guilt, depression and despair for the poor creature. It wasn't his fault, he was a loving companion during the hard times his master suffered. Dex did nothing wrong but he was going to be left behind as this guy moved on with his life, left for dead because Greg was now bored with him.

So I waited patiently for a few months whilst I scoped out this guy's place. Some visions are strong and accurate - for instance I could pinpoint the exact street and house from the flashes of detail afforded to me - but timeframes are never easy to pin down.

I was waiting for Dex to be relegated to the garden every time Greg entertained his women, so I had to persevere and scope out the place for a while, but eventually it happened.

One dingy October night I snuck down the alley behind the row of houses where Greg resided, and peered over the fence to see poor old Dex cowering on his cardboard bed, whilst the rain began to fall.

I know what some of you may be thinking; I'm a thief, a dog-napper; I should have alerted the authorities. Yeah ok, maybe, but I didn't. Instead I prized open the bottom of the fence with a small hammer and out popped Dex without any hesitation or reluctance.

He sprung from the gap in the fence like a released convict and immediately jumped at me, pinning me to the floor and licking my face loving. So excited and overjoyed was he at seeing me, he even pissed a little on my jeans!

Instantly I knew I was doing the right thing and that this abandoned dog would change my life, that Dex would live a happy and fulfilled life with me instead of being consigned to roam the streets.

Without being led or coaxed, he followed me as I got to my feet, left the alley and jumped into my truck. Without hesitation he leapt onto the passenger side seat as I opened the door for him. Then sat there watching the traffic and the world go by as we travelled home, tail wagging and tongue dangling the whole way.

Sometimes I think I was *meant* to rescue Dex; I was *meant* to see Greg's future and act upon it; we were *meant* to form a strong and lifelong bond. I often think fate brought us together then I remember I don't really believe in that.

I often wonder how Greg reacted once/if he discovered his dog had escaped? Maybe he cared? Maybe he cried? Perhaps he noticed? Maybe all of these things, but I never saw a lost dog poster or any evidence that he tried to track his dog down.

So I am not that bad after all, am I? I am a good guy.

Oh and later I found out that Dex can predict cancer, but that's another story for another day.

# Chapter 6

Tomorrow now and I'm back at the fair setting up for the coming day's trade, its 10am and the fair is just springing into life, as I make my way through it. It's technically open, seeing as it's on a large public space, but not much is happening and there are no real punters to be seen, just curious passersby. Things will get pretty wild later as the hours tick on and the Friday night revellers appear - it's the penultimate day of the event so trade should be busy. This just so happens to be one of the biggest travelling fairs in Europe, and pitches up here for a week every summer, during which I can earn a enough to sustain me during the lean winter months.

It's not particularly seasonal the psychic game, but I'm pretty lazy so I tend to slack off a bit during the cold winter months. I will seek out other large fairs and events to fill the gaps, but only sporadically. Otherwise you can spend numerous days and nights on the road, sleeping in your van and pissing in hedgerows. It's massively unglamorous and a huge endurance test, if I try to fill my diary, so I pick and choose - some corporate work, some conventions, private readings, the odd private party - I've got myself a unique and alternate career. A fairly lonely and strange existence, but it's all I got at the minute and this annual event makes all the difference with its huge crowds, familiar faces and old friends.

It's really a monster this one - a 40 acre site with over 300 attractions and over 100 rides - and over the years it's built up a nice community feel. I'm a resolute loner, but the friends I do have are on the circuit and I see them here every year.

Such is the size of this thing that some of the families travel with it, as it heads into Europe. Something I've always threatened to do but the language barrier is a bit of a problem - can't really predict someone's future if you can't speak their language now can you? Plus I'm not a traveller, and it's not in my genes to live on the road like others can.

The hardened fair families live on site in their caravans and haul these massive rigs and rides miles around the continent. The real hardcore put their kids into a winter school, and during the summer the little ones are given study packs to work on whilst on the road. There are often study sessions and teachings on site for these travelling kids.

It takes extreme commitment that kind of lifestyle, and I've real admiration for the ones that can stick to it. Me, as I said, I just sit around during the winter, doing the odd private and corporate event until the summer comes back around - I'm far too lazy to do that kind legwork.

Corporate events are always a good little earner during the festive period, and are usually a mixture of fun, pity, and general futility. More often than not at such an event, everyone is far too inebriated to actually listen to what I'm telling them - I'm just a sideshow to an evening of drinking and inappropriate flirting. I usually have a long line of dull and mundane office monkeys, with little or no personality and only a slither of a life outside the workplace. All of them have families, mortgages, 9-5's and pensions in their futures and the mendacity of such an existence always leaves me baffled. Why commit to a lifetime of hard work to that kind of existence? Why bother?

But that's just a different kind of dedicated lifestyle that I'm too lazy to indulge in.

I stroll serenely past a broken down thrill ride and can hear a heated debate between two carnies, as they slave over a busted ride component. Something's not working right and there are tools, rags, dirty hands and frustrated faces on display. It's easy to forget, but it really is quite the feat of engineering getting this all set up. I just roll up to my spot the day before opening, and by then hours of set-up work have taken place. Little attractions like mine are just window dressing and filler in amongst the thrill rides and mobile structures.

Most of the big rides morph and transform from a huge HGV trailer into a fully-fledged fairground attraction. It can be incredible to see a dingy and boring 18 wheeler wagon become a tower drop ride almost instantly.

The preparation and sheer hard work involved to transform such machines is mind-blowing, teams of spend hours erecting, building, tweaking and testing such rides. That's all before there given a final polish and clean before any punter ever sees it or the fair's even open for trade. This is no 3 rides for a tenner, wristband entry, based in a car park fairground - this is the real deal. This has history and heritage behind it - this fair is famous.

Along with the modern thrill-seeking stuff that you find everywhere, it still has some old school steam driven rides -

even some old fashioned attractions like the wall of death, hall of mirrors and penny arcades. There's even a carousel that dates back to 1881 apparently!

Despite all of this, the preparation, the care, the love some people have for these machines and this way of life, I've seen and heard of some horrible things happening at these types of fairs. Accidents do, and will happen - more regularly than you would expect or hope - and a missed nut or a loose bolt can have huge repercussions.

Here are some accidents and problems that I've seen/or heard about over the years:

Bolts coming loose

Sometimes this can be nothing other than a small bolt shaking loose, often whilst packing up at the end of a stint, they will discover numerous bolts under a ride, hidden from view after they drop loose. The vast majority of the time there are little to no consequences. After all there are hundreds of bolts on each of these things and there not all critical to the structural makeup - but some are.

There's this one story of a bolt coming loose from the gondola of a ferries wheel. This particular gondola was at the peak of the wheel at the time, obviously this bolt was holding it up there. People fell. People died. I wasn't there and I didn't see it so it could just be an urban legend. Maybe?

Much more common are bolts flying from a spinning machine and hitting things. Like a bullet from a gun, a bolt coming loose from a whirling ride can cause much destruction. Most of the time they will hit the actual rides themselves and the various surroundings and furniture. No big deal. Sometimes though, they can hit people. They have stuck passers-by, spectators, and people actually on the rides - sometimes even people queuing. They have cut and scarred people, they have broken bones, and they have caused many a medical emergency, and even a couple of lawsuits.

Faulty wiring

Electrical faults happen regularly. Rides short out and stop mid-flow, rides malfunction, fuses blow, motors burn out etc. People get stuck on rides during power cuts and electrical breakdowns, rides gets closed altogether, the odd generator blows up. All the typical problems you would expect from such an operation.

There is this one story though of electrical shocks being caused to everyone in a particular ride queue. Someone wasn't paying much attention whilst hooking up the ride and left an earth wire directly under a steel railing. No one really noticed until the ride was fired up and the first set of punters all received small electric shocks upon touching the handrails. Free rides were given out in compensation.

Collisions

Some particular types of rides spin and twirl outwards at speed, and every now and then the perimeter barriers will be set up to tightly. If tested properly beforehand, this will be picked up instantly, but a few times I've seen rides striking barriers when full with punters. Such barriers can creep a few meters here and there over the course of the stay, and collisions do happen if they migrate too much. Never much more than a load clatter and slight distress to the riders though.

Swing rides

These things can be particularly dangerous given the rather primitive set-up and minimal harnessing. We've all seen them - single person seats that spin around a big carousel that gradually rises higher, forcing the seat and riders outwards at an angle. It's a fairly sedate ride for youngsters normally, but the amount of issue with them is startling.

Numerous times people have fallen out of the chairs, mainly due to rider tampering and the sheer fact that it's only really a piece of string holding you in, sometimes a thin chain.

One time a ride didn't quite lower back to ground level properly at the end and everyone jumped out thinking the ground was immediately below them. It wasn't and they all fell a few feet to the ground. It was mildly amusing. One other time the back of one of these seats separated and the rider had a nasty fall backwards, off the spinning chair.

Another time someone hit the emergency stop button whilst the ride was in full flow - momentum sending everyone crashing nastily into the riders ahead of them.

There was also that one time I heard about, when a young child decided to stand up at the peak of the ride - he was thrown, dart like, from the ride. Tears, recriminations and a hospital trip followed.

Go-Karts

Not surprisingly accidents are practically part and parcel of the go-karting experience, most of the time it's just simple collisions, kart toppling, flips or collisions with the barriers that cause the drama. Pretty standard stuff, but there was that one time a woman apparently got her long ponytail caught up in the engine behind her seat.

She was scalped mid race. Again I wasn't there and I didn't witness it so it could just be an urban legend? Maybe?

The fair is a much more dangerous place to be than what most people would like to believe, but I'd better stop there because I don't want to put you off coming.

Due to the size of this one, it's become a smorgasbord of old and new fashion rides, complimented with the usual off beat attractions, and is divided into sections.

The traditional, old fashioned steam stuff is grouped together with its associated attractions like the wall of death. It's a beautiful area, like something out of a museum or a 40's American movie. It is drowned in the customary accordion music typical for a fairground of its time and era. It's a harmonious, intriguing and antique like space that harks back to a more innocent and respectful time. Alongside this classy Eden sits the modern rides and arcades you see everywhere, complete with thumping drum and bass soundtrack and copious bright lighting. All the excess, exuberance and energy you expect from the ADD, status updating, energy drinking, youth of today.

There is actually a section were these two worlds intertwine, you're in the past and the future at the same time, a slither of area where dance music abuses one ear lobe whilst classical stuff tingles at the other.

Accompanying those two polarizing spaces you have a large perimeter of food stalls and stands, all offering the typical standard fair treats alongside a strange selection of street and foreign foods. Hot digs, burgers, chips, pizza's etc, the list is endless but every taste is catered for. I'm pretty sure you can get and Sushi somewhere here, if you fancy mixing thrill rides with raw fish?

Filling up the rest of the site are all the miscellaneous attractions and games you would expect. Including the ones that are impossible to win at, but seemingly irresistible to punters who desperately need that tacky stuffed animal. The coconut shies, the basketball hoops, ring the bottle, hook the duck etc… All of these are virtually impossible to win and are heavily stacked in the tradesman's favour – I'll share some tricks of the trade, but not just yet.

I wander through the bustle and rising hubbub of a fairground springing into life slowly, savouring the crisp and bright morning as I go. I'm pitched nicely in the old fashion area, a sensible place for me as aesthetically it makes sense, but also positions me perfectly within my older target market.

There can be a wide and diverse range of punters that attend such a large and famous fair. Such is the sheer size of the thing that people travel from far and wide to soak up the atmosphere, and be overcharged for old fashioned entertainment. Aside from fanatic fair followers and tourists, there is a perfect cross section of society here every day. Pensioners, families, mature couples, young and married couples, teenagers, children, professionals, alcoholics, drug addicts etc, etc. Such is the sheer size and diversity of entertainment on offer there really is something for everyone - and indeed everyone seems to show up. It's the perfect crowd and everyone trader seems to find their niche.

Mine tends to be 30+ folk. Teenagers and youngster aren't really interested in the traditional side of the fair, and typically, don't give two hoots about their futures either. I read very few sub 30 year olds. I snare the older gentlemen and women, the mature adults who have long since lost the bravado and zest of youth, and the middle-aged folk who are concerned about pensions and job security. The people ensnared by a 30 year mortgage they may never see the back of. These people are concerned about the future - not the 20 something's who are consumed by their genitals.

I lease up Dex outside the van and unload my sandwich board. This is what is says:

The Great Psy Paxley

Savant, mystic, psychic and fortune teller

Your future - today!

£15 per reading

This is it - the full extent of my advertising.

I have to call myself Psy because no-one is going to go see a psychic called Bill, it's just not jazzy enough. Not enough mystery in that name to inspire and attract. It's a granddad, old man's name - not a name that will conjure intrigue and a sense of mystery about me as a unique person.

See this is all about presentation - I need to look and feel the part to convince these people. A psychic needs that air of mystery, that feeling of otherworldliness; I need to give off a feeling of the unknown and unpredictability. I can't just be a normal person with a normal name, and I just can't wear jeans and a t-shirt either. Thus, the renaming and my customary performance gear - tall Top hat, cloak and waistcoat, simple white shirt underneath and large leather boots. I look a bit like Jack the Ripper.

I can pull off the presentation stuff so the advert only really details the price. People can see the ornate gypsy van, the clobber and the paraphernalia; they know what's going on in this particular corner of the fair so I don't need to push too hard. It's all a bit cliché, but they get the gist. People love clichés.

Plus it seems to work - on a good day I can get through 30+ readings. I can take home over 3k for the week, if I work hard and the weather is kind.

Right now the suns shining and the fair seem to be filling slowly. I crack open a beer and sit with Dex, waiting the first days reading.

## A Reading

We have a man in his early 60's, smartly dressed in shorts and a polo shirt, a handsome silver fox. The sheer class and heft of the watch he hands me tells me this is an affluent man who has done well and retired early. He looks well off and has the kind of skin and tanned complexion that suggests he regularly holidays in the south of France.

Despite this, he is anxious and unsettled as he sits opposite me, waiting for me to dispense information. I can feel he is wrestling with a big decision that he somehow expects me to answer.

I focus hard and see the following.

I see him on a sail boat with a wife of at least 10 years his senior. I see them sailing across the channel in brilliant sunshine on his large sailing boat. I see them sipping champagne and eating caviar on the deck. He is living the dream and enjoying the fruits of a smart business career.

I see him call his mother one evening. I see him crying down the phone as his senile mother struggles to remember who her sons are. She is in the throes of dementia and seeing out her days in a budget nursing home.

*I see him crippled with guilt. I see him consoled by his botoxed spouse.*

*I see a storm set in as they sail further towards the horizon. The waves are huge and life threatening. He is concerned, because he has limited experience on the open ocean and he is concerned because his mother is dying whilst he battles these raging storms.*

*Outside the cabin window, I can see the violent black sea swirling around his tiny boat. The sky is pitched black and the waves are furious. Rain is lashing at the boat at a near horizontal trajectory as it is driven by the vicious gales. The boat and its passengers are being tossed around the unforgiving ocean like a plastic bag in the wind. This is the kind of storm that kills people. The kind of situation you never really live to tell of - people die when Mother Nature behaves like this.*

*Inside the helpless vessel he thinks karma is about to kill him for abandoning his mother to set sail with his young girlfriend. I see him call his mother as a 10 foot wave lashes the boat. There is no answer.*

*Flash forward and I see them at his mother's funeral some*

*time later. He is being scowled at by several other people who appear to be siblings. See they carried the burden of their mother's demise whilst he topped up his tan and had sex with his new trophy wife. He has paid for the funeral out right, but it is out of guilt and it shows on his face.*

*He is grief stricken and sick to his stomach.*

*I see his buxom wife leaving him several months later because he's not much fun anymore. The grief, the stress, the mourning, has added years to him and he no longer looks vibrant and energetic like he did when they met. She runs off with someone 10 years his junior and it breaks his heart. He had his fun and it cost him.*

*I see all this and yet I struggle to give him any kind of meaningful reading. What am I supposed to say? Don't be seduced by pretty divorcees - Don't follow your dream of sailing the channel - Don't leave your mother's side until she is dead.*

*I can't say any of these things to him so I feed him vague platitudes.*

*'You must follow your heart but keep in mind those who are most important to you,'*

'You must put your family at the forefront of your priorities and treasure every day with them,'

'You have earned the right to enjoy your remaining years but beware of pending responsibilities.'

I say vague things like this that could mean go sailing and say at home at the same time.

I tell him everything without telling him anything.

He leaves as confused and agitated as he was when he arrived. He is consoled by a pretty 40 something blonde, as he leaves the sitting.

## Chapter 7

Alice is the kind of girl guys like me dreams of. In fact I spend most of the year doing just that - dreaming and waiting for the fair to roll back into town. She's a pretty, curvaceous, energetic, adventurous and naïve young blonde princess, whom is part of the fair community.

She travels with it throughout Europe with her family, which consists of her, two wild brothers, and her disabled father. These two Wall of Death riding brothers simultaneously both hate my guts, and are not shy in showing it - they hate me because Alice doesn't. The dad seems a stern and controlling type also, but he tends to keep his distance so I don't think he hates me as much as his sons?

For some reason, reasons I don't want to delve too deeply into, Alice seems to enjoy my sullen and bitter company. We have a kind of on-off-on again type thing going. Not a Hollywood, Rom-Com type thing, just two people who enjoy each other's company for a week or so every year. Every time the fair is in town we reacquaint ourselves with each other and do the dating thing.

I like her because she's 10 years my junior and a

stunningly beautiful young lady, and she likes me because….? I've no real ideal why, but I guess she likes older men? Older, mysterious, men who have pet Alsatians and the kind of rough and ready appearance you see in westerns.

   She has told me it's partly because I'm not like all the other guys she encounters. Every day she has guys trying it on with her whilst she's just trying to serve up a burger and chips. No one is in the mood for being wooed when they are frying bacon - especially when they are all far too desperate to get into her pants and clumsy about showing it.

   Truth is, I'm just as desperate, but I'm just far more subtle about it.

   Anyway Alice wants to leave the fair lifestyle behind one day to study fashion in London. I hope she does because the fair may be many things, but a prosperous career path it isn't.

   What exactly keeps her here I'm not too sure, because she's in her mid-20's and needs no-one's permission, although family commitment being what they are, I guess she can't really just up and leave. Also part of me thinks she's too scared of rejection to take the exams and go through the application process.

Her brothers are a particular problem too.

When they were young, their mother was taken from them during Alice's birth and their father also paralysed himself from the waist down when she was young. A nasty fall from one of the rides he was trying to repair; he was constructing one of the tower cranes with no protective harnessing and fell 30 feet, he's been wheelchair bound since. Consequently he travels with the family, but rarely leaves the caravan - leaving the two brothers as protectors in chief, strict guardians of their slim, fun loving sister.

Many a black eye and bruised rib have been dished out by them over the years as Alice has slowly aged, gradually garnering more and more attention from the punters as she matured.

I mention her because it's almost 11pm, the fair is closing up for the night - council curfew regarding noise spoiling the fun - and I'm heading over to her stall to see if she fancies a nightcap.

It's been a busy and productive day and I've had an interesting parade of customers. I told a middle aged woman that she will one day fulfil her dream of motherhood, despite foreseeing a doctor telling her she is barren. I told a younger women that her lover will still be waiting for her upon her return from a lengthily study trip, despite seeing the fallout from his infidelity. I told an old gentleman that he must enjoy his remaining time, because I saw him having a stroke in the near future.

I saw a lot of sadness today and dished out a lot of false hope. I told a lot of lies because I can't bring myself to do anything else. Fate is a cruel mistress and little old me can't do anything about it.

This gift has gotten to be soul destroying and it's only the thought of Alice that gets me through sometimes. I button up my trench coat and head out into the emptying fair. All around me attractions are closing up and punters are heading off into the night, a sea of rubbish and much misspent cash left behind.

The only thing still in operation is the Wall of Death. On its final show and heading towards its thrilling finale, a crowd of remaining punters enjoying the show inside as me and Dex amble past. It's deafening roar filling the night.

I have to be very careful because, as I said, I don't get along with her brother, thus - I take my chance to approach Alice when their still riding, ensuring they will be preoccupied and I won't be attack today.

They really hate me you see. I'm too old for her, I'm a weirdo with no prospects, I can't provide for her, I'm a loser with unkempt hair and no abs etc. All of the above is true of course, but you tell a girl what she can't have and she will just pursue it more vigorously.

I should thank them really; they help to keep things fresh and edgy between us. We don't exactly sneak around but there is certainly a element of stealth to our meetings. Without their overbearing presence and protectiveness she may have got bored a long time ago.

She's just cleaning up the grill when I get to her stand. Rose above the ground slightly in her trailer, she stands behind a hot griddle all day dispensing burgers, chips, bacon rolls, drinks etc. She hasn't got the worst job at the fair, but she's not far from it. The litter pickers, security guards and health and safety officers have more tedium, abuse and grime to deal with, but not much more. Despite this she carries it out with gusto and the enthusiasm of youth.

Alice is every bit a middle aged man's porno dream. She is the naïve and sweet babysitter, the cute and mischievous girl next door, she is the friend of his daughter who is irresistible and naughty, and she is the schoolgirl desperate for a good grade.

She's a golden haired, blue eyed, size 8 beauty that I would die for. A cute, medium height, slim and sensuous young lady whose body peaks and curves in a perfect formula of sexual attraction.

Oh she's sweet, kind, naïve, funny, enthusiastic and loyal as well.

Looking surprisingly resplendent in her apron and hair net she sees me approaching with Dex by my side and offers a devastating smile.

"Hey Billy", she calls out whilst scrubbing the flat grill top with verve.

I ask her how her day was whilst she passes me a pile of leftover chips from the fryer, destined for the bin, if I don't eat them up.

"Oh you know - great really. We took a good few hundred pounds and Janet here got some guys number", she points her dirty scrubbing brush in Janet's direction.

Janet is a 55 year old grandma and works the fair whenever it's in town; she doesn't hear this and continues to cash up in the corner oblivious.

I scoff chips and feed some to Dex as Alice ducks down below the counter to salvage some cleaning fluid.

I ask her if she fancies a nightcap.

"A nightcap Billy, I know what that means - hanging around in you flat watching terrible films before having sex", she smiles, squirting soap across the flat grill top.

I tell her that's exactly what it means unless she wants to go to a bar or something.

"Jeez I'd love to Billy, but my brothers will be here any minute and they want me to help them with the pack down preparations before tomorrow's last show." she continues, commencing scrubbing once again.

I'm gutted, but won't let it show - must not appear too desperate.

I tell her Ok but we better do something tomorrow seeing as it's the last day of the fair and all.

"Yeah sure babe, but you better take me out then. I don't want to sit around you flat. Take me out into town before I leave in a few days. Treat me like a princess eh?" she says as smiles at me seductively.

A smile so perfect and sweet, I would take her anywhere, and give her anything just to see it again.

I tell her it will be the greatest night of her life as Dex finishes off the last of the stale chips.

Off in the distance the deafening engines that accompany her brother's day job come to an end and punters start to trail out of the arena. Realising her brothers could now show up at any minute, I tell her I'll see her tomorrow night then.

"You know it", she replies, leaning over the stand and giving me a soft peck on the lips.

I scurry off into the darkness leaving her to work on into the night. Savouring the aftermath of her soft, peach like lips as I make my way home, I'm now faced with the task of living up to my promise. This young girl needs some entertaining tomorrow night. I'd better get my beauty sleep.

# Chapter 8

Later the next night, and I've already taken Alice on the night of her dreams as promised. The night of her dreams began with a classic 2 for £10 chain pub dinner, she had a lasagne - I had a mixed grill, we ordered cheesy garlic bread on the side and two pints of standard larger. It all cost less than £20 and tasted like it.

After that I took her to the cinema next door, watched some superhero nonsense, touched her up in the back row, then we ended back at my 1 bed paradise.

Currently I'm in bed, it's late / early, and Alice is draped across me, snoozing with her head on my chest. We've had sex a couple of time since getting in and are both spent. Lust has been replaced with fatigue. It's not easy keeping up with a young lady almost half your age but somehow I seem to manage it.

Despite all that activity I'm struggling to sleep, as the moonlight beams in through the open curtains. My single bedroom is small and sparsely furnished with a simple metal framed bed, topped with a tired mattress, a cheap flat pack wardrobe and a chest of drawers with a small TV atop. I often struggle to sleep and the cheap plastic box offers some vague comfort and distraction on such nights.

Right now is one such occasion as I lay in bed, post coitus, smothered by Alice's comatose body, as someone tries to flog me something on the shopping channel in mute. It appears to be an incredibly lightweight, flexible and revolutionary hosepipe that will apparently change my life; A steal at £55, Postage and packaging and additional £6.99.

I would turn it over, but the remote has been discarded across the floor in our flurried love making and Alice seems so sweet, so peaceful, seemingly dreaming happily, I'm loathed to move and wake her.

I lie awake, bathed in the moonlight, distracted by the man talking silently on the box in the corner.

Right now I feel all of these things; happy, content, tired, restless, agitated, lucky, pensive, pessimistic and ever so slightly dirty.

I feel like the luckiest man alive to have this beauty with me, but on edge because every time we have sex I panic it could be the last time, that a young hunk is just around the corner and my charms will instantly fade when compared.

I'm very much a glass half empty kind of guy; A guy who

waits for his life to crumble around him and expects shit to hit the fan at every turn. Living for the moment, because the bad things are just around the corner, desperately trying to enjoy the present, because I've seen the future and it doesn't tend to be pretty. Fate is a cruel mistress and the future everyone wants just doesn't exist.

Alice will leave eventually, I figure, as a lady tries to sell me a mop that will also change my life. Who actually buys this kind of crap in the middle of the night is beyond me?

I'm the guy who had a vision of his mother's heart failure at 17 and didn't know what to do about it. The guy who told his mother this and that I had had this magical vision when sifting through her purse. The guy, who was scolded, ignored and disciplined by his ill mother for attempting to steal some change. I'm the guy who sat at her bedside a few months later and watched the life slowly drain away. I was left to fend for myself whilst still a teenager because dad was long gone.

This is how I first found out I was gifted.

I was too young, too scared and too confused to help my mother then, and not a lot has changed since. I'm still too afraid, too timid, to pessimistic, to see the future and then actually take control of it - fate is what it is and there is no fighting it.

The future controls me. My visions control me.

A man now pops on the TV and seems to be holding some kind of magical wash cloth. So magical is it that for just £10.99 this thing will remove caked on grim and dirt with a single swipe. This is revolutionary technology apparently - in a dish cloth for £10.99.

I try hard to sleep but my mind refuses. I try to savour the moment, but my mind keeps harassing me with distant memories that I'd rather forget. Like the time I tried to tell a customer that his kidney is due to fail and that he needs to track down his long lost son for a donor. I tried to intervene after seeing this man wasting away on the transplant list because he was too stubborn to reconcile with his progeny.

Like the first time I saw Dex rubbing his face on a customer and not realising what it meant. It was a young toddler who had stopped to pet him and his stare meant nothing to me then. That was until I read her parent's future and saw her shaven head in it as they watched her drift away in the cancer ward.

   I was a young guy who was perpetually confused and terrified. I didn't know what any of this meant or what exactly I had access to for a long time. It took many, many, correct predictions for me to finally accept my talents as anything more than just a mental problem.

   I now accept I can see the future, but I still don't know how to act on it or control such information. Every attempt I've ever made to try and intervene and guide people has backfired badly - that's why I never say anything anymore. I just let fate do its thing.

   I now accept that I will say goodbye to Alice at some point and the future might not be that great - or it could be incredible? I don't know because I'm too afraid to read myself. I now accept that I know nothing and everything at the same time, I'm a savant and completely useless all at once.

   One thing is for sure, I need this washcloth because it just cleaned a greasy oven dish in a few elegant swipes!

# Chapter 9

How they rip you off at the fair part 1 - The claw grabber.

These come in numerous shapes and sizes and contain anything from a standard cuddly toy to a watch with money taped around the outside a the box. Mainly they contain any in vogue cuddly toy, one that's likely to attract the kids and induce the nagging power they possess; sometimes they have watches, MP3 players, phones, or other such electronics goods to entice the older punters.

Once in Japan I saw one with live crabs in! Live crabs swimming around peacefully in a decent sized aquarium, only for a giant mechanical crane to drop down and grab at their legs. Then those crazy Japanese eat them straight out of the machine of course! I spent several million Yen playing this machine so I could win one of these poor creatures and subsequently release it into a nearby river. I'm an animal lover, what can I say?

The name of the game is to use the crane controls to guide a mechanical claw around the small enclosure and, when hovering enticingly over a desired toy, press the big red drop button. The claw drops around your target and the arms *should* close around it and lift your prize into the air, eventually dropping it into the prize bucket back at the claws starting point as it completes its journey. Only problem is that this rarely happens.

We've all been duped into these, most of us on regular and re-occurring occasions. For my sins I often sink a few quid into these things for no apparent reason, just hoping that a tacky cuddly toy will be mine! Perhaps it's the sense of achievement or accomplishment, the thrill of success and victory? Perhaps some people really want that stuffed dog? A lot of guys seem to try and impress women with such machines only to come up red faced and poorer.

See these machines are actually straight up cons. They are programmed and designed to fail the vast majority of the time. The profitability of these arcade monstrosities are based upon the fact that only 1 in 5, 1 in 10, 1 in 20 times, will the claws actually operate efficiently and allow you to win a prize.

Encased within the makeup of these units, somewhere behind the coin slot, is a small box with two dials on it. One controls the pressure applied by the claw and the other controls the win ration. Obviously the dials are stacked heavily against you so the claw will not exert enough pressure to grab your toy property and when it does, this will be every 10, 20 or if you're lucky 5, attempts.

What makes this even trickier is that every time the 1 in 20 rolls around, you still have to ensure your aim is good and the claw is in the optimum position to allow it to work its magic. You could spurn your chance if your aim is off or you're over ambitious with your choice.

So how do you beat these things?

It's either by sheer luck or science.

You could, and people regularly will, get lucky without knowing how these things work and walk away with a pink elephant. After all people carrying these things around the fair with them is effective advertising for the games. As it is with all fairground prize games - some people will be allowed to win to entice passers-by to partake, it proves whatever you're up against isn't impossible. Sheer chance X numbers of goes, a lot of people get lucky because virtually everyone seems to have at least one go. So you could chuck £20 in and hope you get it right when the chance rolls around. Or you can play the waiting game, play the science card, and partake in a little observational experiment.

It takes patience, more than is really feasible to win such a poultry prize, but if you stand and watch you can work out the win ration.

Pick a machine. Wait for someone to win. Keep watching and count the number of goes before someone wins again and there's your ration. Now keep watching and jump on when the cycle is about to repeat and the winning turn is due. Of course you still have to aim well and hit your target, but at least you will know the machine is on your side if you do.

So much money is wasted when the machine has no intention of gripping properly or playing fair, these things litter the fairgrounds, and their profitability is huge compared to other attractions because of this.

Other tips include never going for a concealed or blocked prize for obvious reasons, why make it harder by having other toys blocking you way? Also never play a machine that is overstocked and full, such machines are probably very high in the ration odds and offer little in the way of wins. You want a sparse, clear machine that will allow a good full grip around your chosen target when you seize your chance.

Now whether anyone really has the patience, need, or desire to hang around watching a machine endlessly and counting the failed attempts is another matter, is a fluffy toy cat really worth the hours of research? But these are some of the biggest cons on the fair ground, and it's the only sure fire way to stack the odds in your favour, so you do the leg work or you take a mindless punt.

    Don't say I didn't warn you.

## Chapter 10

It's the next day now and there's a guy sat in front of me that is really giving me the creeps. I'm not sure why, but there is something extremely unnerving and unsettling about him.

He looks like any other middle aged man you would encounter in an insurance firm or mundane office job. Smartly dressed in a cheap suit, balding on top with an ever expanding waistline, he is very much the archetype middle manager. A hard working, but uninspiring individual who has no doubt committed years of his life to a career and a job that no-one gives two shits about. He answers his phone during out of work hours, never takes all of his allotted holiday allowance, and often shows up unannounced in the office whilst he's supposed to be on leave - That kind of guy.

He's a dull and average man in every sense of the word, but he's really unsettling me. There was something about the way he came in and sat down for this reading that just doesn't sit well with me. Like he's about to take a lie detector test or sit an exam, like he feels on trial just being here. I can feel a damaged individual somewhere beneath the frumpy surface.

He is calm and patient, but tense and edgy at the same time. Behind his blank and deep stare I can feel something vacant, something numb and dangerous. He feels like a man on the edge, a coiled spring, and that my reading could just push him beyond.

I've sat opposite a lot of people but this guy really feels different.

I swallow hard and ask for his watch. A black leather strap and plane faced piece that suggests wealth without the need to advertise it.

"Be careful with that – it's more precious to me than anything else in the world," he whispers as I take it from him. All the while he is staring deep into my eyes in what I'm sure is an attempt to purvey threat.

I tell him it will be in safe hands as a shiver rolls down my spine, confused as to what exactly he means by that, and terrified by his unsettling tone.

I start to focus and suddenly everything becomes clear and I see things that I have never seen before.

First I see this guy leaving his house, his wife slamming the door behind him. He is off on another business trip to the south coast and she isn't happy about it. She says he cares more for his job than he does his family. I see her having sex with a younger more attractive man whilst he is gone.

Flash forward and she is leaving him. He is too boring and career focused for her. She has a new toy boy lover and she's not attracted to our guy anymore. She takes the kids with her to stay at her mums.

I see him have a breakdown that night.

I see him wake up with a sex worker in his bed. She has bruises on her face and our guy has to tip her excessively just to stop her calling the police.

I see him sat in a doctor's surgery alone, crying his eyes out at the news offered up by the physician.

Later now and I see him sat in a van outside of a shopping mall, watching intently as his wife enters alone. I see her shopping for lingerie as he trails her from afar, its Christmas and she has a saucy surprise in store for her toy boy. I see our guy stride into the shop after her. He has a gun concealed in his coat pocket and he prods it into his ex-wife's back.

Moments later I see him lead her out of the shop by the arm, gun pressed into her back and concealed the entire time. She is distraught, but too afraid to raise the alarm. Our guy is muttering stuff about making her pay and getting his revenge. Years of pent up hostility have burst to the surface.

Flash to him throwing his wife into the back of a white transit van. The van has a homemade bomb in it. He makes his ex-wife sit amongst the barrels of fertiliser and acid whilst he clutches a detonator and screams profanities at her through tears filled eyes.

Later now and I see rubble.

I see carnage. I see the effect this huge homemade bomb will have on the local shopping mall.

I see bodies - lots of bodies.

I see piles of shattered glass and rubble.

I see people running and screaming from the mall in mortal fear for their lives.

I see a massacre at Christmas. I see Santa's grotto showered in rubble. The bomb was in an underground parking lot and has torn a porthole of carnage up through the centre of the shopping mall.

I see the corpses of shoppers scattered across the tiled floors, I see blood pooling everywhere and snaking along the patterns in these tiles. People are bleeding and dying right there outside Top shop.

I have several very specific vision of the destruction in quick succession, montage format if you will. I see a mother cradling her young boy in her arms and seeking desperate help after some shrapnel lodged itself into his abdomen; I see a row of bodies lined neatly across the ground floor in a bizarre line after the explosion caused everyone travelling on a third floor escalator to tumble to their deaths over the handrail; I see a security guard feeling blindly for his radio whilst dust and debris consume his vision; I see what could be a doll, perhaps a real baby, crushed under a slab of concrete - two tiny legs poking out from under the grey monolith.

It is a cold, overcast and drizzly day and the explosion, having blown out the glass atrium, has caused rain to fall heavily indoors. Some of this may also be water from burst water pipes.

I see what looks like a war zone in all but setting.

Clothes, gifts, trinkets, jewellery, electronics - every perceivable consumer product is scattered amongst the bodies, the blood and the debris.

People are fighting for their lives on Christmas Eve.

Cut to the car park and I see the mangled carcass of the white van that once held our man and his ex-wife. They have both died in the explosion. Our man has taken his own life along with many, many others.

The level that once held this parked van has collapsed down onto the lower floors. This car park now resembles a scrap yard, with cars displaced from the upper layers, resting precariously atop others.

Some of these cars have corpses in them.

It's later now and I see the emergency services fighting a blaze that has broken out post explosion. See our man positioned his van to blow straight through the air condition system for the mall and caused a resultant gas leak and fire. Later again and a roof collapses in the blaze and takes the life of two firemen.

A day later the headlines are damming; The worst terror attack in British history - Great Britain's 9/11 - England's Lockerbie. The headlines are lazy but the shock that the nation is feeling is well portrayed.

Two days later, and the Prime minister is on the TV. He tells everyone that terror will not win. No one believes him.

A week later we have remarkable survival stories as the young and old alike are pulled from the rubble. Still just about alive, a young child becomes the poster boy for the tragedy as he is photographed still clutching his beloved blue bear after several days buried in darkness.

The same week stories are dredged up about the attacker. His name is Phillip. He was a mild mannered insurance manager. He was a member of the local neighbourhood watch committee. There are several stunned neighbours interviewed whom detail how normal, nice and approachable our man is.

No one reports a monster.

A month later now, the shopping centre, with deep structural damage is condemned to demolition. The costs run into the millions. The death toll has topped 100.

Our man, the guy sat opposite me as I clutch his cheap but precious watch, is a monster on an Osama Bin Laden scale. I have never seen anything like this before and I am left stunned and distraught by the visions.

The sound of his tidy watch bouncing off the table jolts me back into the room as it slips from my fraught grip, such is the power of what I have seen I am physically trembling and startled.

Aghast and speechless I stare across the small table at Phil, our would-be terrorist. This man, this smartly dressed, mundane looking gentleman, is destined to commit mass murder on a scale unprecedented in this country. His black eyes piece my soul and I think he can tell I've seen something unspeakable.

His face is an unnerving mix of calm and patience that is all the more unsettling now the full details have shown themselves to me. He reaches across the table suddenly after his watch. So suddenly I lurch backwards and tumble from my chair, terrified and fearful for my life.

He retrieves his watch calmly from the table and gets to his feet. As he stands above me, I see once again the stacked bodies of his victims; the trails of blood and the tears of the victims, the countless masses of mourners, the sea of commemorative flowers at the site, the monument erected in their honour many months later.

I see all of this in the eyes of this 5'7' overweight, balding man as he offers me a hand to help me to my feet. I am a trembling wreck on the floor of my caravan as he grabs me by the arm and hauls me to my feet against my will. His touch is cold, warm, forceful and submissive all at once. The touch of a man who has two sides, two faces and two personalities, the touch of a family man, and terrorist at the same time.

"Are you ok, you look like you've seen a ghost?" he inquires as I desperately try to straighten up and regain composure.

I tell him I'm fine and that I cannot carry on with the reading. Apologies, but I have been desperately unwell for the past few days, food poisoning I posit through chattering teeth.

He knows I'm lying, but he accepts his refund without incident as I virtually push him out of the door.

I send him on his way and watch this monster wander

aimlessly and slightly confused into the fair. He disappears from sight behind the carousel and fades into the crowds.

   I stumble back into the caravan and slump onto the floor. I have seen something that I will never be able to un-see. I am forever changed. My initial concern and discomfort with this guy was more than justified - he will kill a lot of people before this year is out.

   He will destroy numerous lives and wreak havoc on the good people of this country. That man - that forgettable bald man with a dull and unattractive demeanour. This man, who just wandered unseen into the assembled crowds, will blow a hole in the earth.

   There is a sleeping monster amongst us and he is going to wake up soon.

   I look down at Dex and he has crawled under the caravan for safety.

## Chapter 11

I sink two cans of larger within minutes of slumping back in the caravan. I have unleashed Dex and bought him in; he was also trembling in fear. He has been replaced with a back in 10 type sign. I need some time to compose myself, some time to think.

I am not the type of person that should be privileged with such information. I am not a reasonable or sensible enough to deal with this. I know not what to do with this information? Never before, have I felt the consequences so harshly of my inherent gift, never before have I seen pile of dead bodies in the future of a client.

With Dex sat beside me I stroke him with one hand and drink with the other in a desperate need to settle our nerves. Phil is gone, but his presence still lingers.

He has instantly put me in a state of perpetual angst. I take a series of deep, intentionally long breaths and slowly composure finds me once more. Right now I feel the following things; fear, terror, despair, futility, responsibility, excitement, dread and adrenaline. I feel like the world has just fallen upon my shoulders and I'm such a coward, I immediately start to think how I can pass this on? Who can I displace this hot potato too? How quickly can my sloped shoulders make this someone else's problem?

I have a series of options as I sit here on the floor of my caravan, 3 cans down now, with a fully grown Alsatian at my side, letting trade pass by outside.

I can tell someone right? Ok but who? Who do I tell this too and how do I break it down?

*'Hi officer I can see the future and this seemingly upstanding man will commit a terrorist act that is unimaginable in a few months' time.'* You think he will believe me? Would you? Do you?

Would you believe the local neighbourhood psychic without a shred of proof or evidence? Would you do anything other than laugh me out of the precinct and probably place me on some kind of list?

I mean, I've never told anyone about my gifts because no one will understand or believe - "*I can see the future.*" - Yeah of course you can! I can hardly expect anyone to take me seriously at the best of times, let alone when I've making such outrageous claims.

I could write some kind of anonymous note I guess, and

post it too the force?

Not the worst ideal in the world but would that be taken seriously? Would it be anything more than a dismissed piece of mail from some local nut?

I very much doubt it. An anonymous letter with this kind of information in may be taken with a hint of caution, due to the extreme nature, but I can't see the local police committing their stretched recourses in the pursuit of a piece of mail. I guess they might put it in some pile and check on it later, or when someone needs something to do. Perhaps they will eventually take it seriously or it may just be put on the backburner until it's too late? After all I assume there just too busy to investigate every single piece of correspondence they receive.

Also in my tiny and pathetic mind, passing on an anonymous note would allow me to forget it entirely. My dumb brain will assume it's all taken care of and that I did the right thing, only for the note to be ignored and the bomb to explode weeks later. Maybe it's time I was a bit more pro-active and forthright? Maybe it's about time I did something for once? Maybe I can tell people but just not yet? I need more evidence, more proof, something to back up the wild claims I will be making, then go to the appropriate people.

Alternately I could intervene.

I could directly go to the guy and try to reason with him. Try to break down, in no uncertain terms, that he is a monster and will kill many innocent people.

Ok, that's crazier than going to the police.

*"Excuse me sir - I can see the future and the other day when I fell over and threw you out without a reading, I had actually seen you commit a massacre on a huge scale. And now I'm here to talk you out of it!"*

Pure insanity!

Plus to be honest the guy is very unsettling. I'm not sure how much more time I could stand to be in his presence. Sure, his exterior is stunningly forgettable and average, but there is just something under the surface that gets to me. I can feel his empathy and humanity fading fast, the hatred and despair replacing it. It gets my spidery senses tingling if you will - this guy feels like my kryptonite.

I can't approach him.

Especially not after the shambolic end to our session, not after I destroyed any credibility and respect he may have had for me. If some stranger came up to me and accused me of such acts, after he had been scrambling around on the floor, I wouldn't be welcoming and clearly this is a guy I do not want to go around upsetting.

I down can number 4 as Dex gets to his feet and paces the van, sniffing the air, looking for something. His actions intrigue me and I watch him blankly as I contemplate doing nothing at all about this.

That's right - nothing!

Let it happen. After all who am I to stand in the way of fate? Who am I to play god in such a way? What gives me the right to meddle in this man's life? I cannot change the future and every time I've tried, I failed miserably.

After all I am no saint, I am not angel, and I'm also no superhero. I'm not in the business of crime fighting, or in a position to join the war on terror. Plus I might just be wrong? This might just be some horrific false alarm? Sure, I've never been wrong before, my visions are always concrete - I CAN see the future - but maybe, just maybe, this time I'm wrong? I'm just a crazy drunk who's delusional? After decades of being right - this time I'm wrong? Could just be?

I may do nothing I reason. Maybe people will die but that is fates card - that is the cards that have been dealt. It's rough, it's tragic and it's horrific, but it is nature's path after all.

I'm not going to do anything I've decided - just sit here and drink my 5$^{th}$ can and hope to forget everything I saw, out of sight - out of mind. As I do this I see Dex, now resting his head on the chair recently occupied by our friend Phil, rubbing its surface with his hairy chin. His big brown eyes are wide and deep as he gazes at me, letting out a low growl as he fixes my gaze. He continues doing this until it finally twigs in my foggy mind what he's trying to tell me.

Phil has cancer.

As I mentioned earlier - Dex can smell cancer, as can all dogs, but what makes him so special is that he can communicate it to me.

And this is how he does it.

He sniffs the person or their recent area, he gazes at me, he lets out a pitying, melancholic, sympathetic growl that is impossible to ignore. The kind of sound that tells you someone's life is in the balance, a noise I've never heard anywhere else before from any other source.

His eyes always full of sorrow and regret as he does this. It's as if he's so loyal to man as a species, that he's already in mourning for the individuals he can tell are terminally ill.

I call him over and pat him gently on the head. I tell him I know what he's trying to tell me. Slowly after hearing this he settles at my side and we both try to relax.

I crack open the 6$^{th}$ can.

Dex has done this twice before. The first time I didn't understand until the kid dropped dead with cancer a few months later. The second time Dex rested his head upon the lap of a young lady as I set up for a reading, rubbing her lovingly whilst groaning at me in the same low frequency tone. Soon after I had a vision of her going through chemo and it all became clear.

Phil will be diagnosed with cancer not long after his wife leaves him and takes the kids. That's why I saw him at the doctors crying. His wife leave - he gets cancer - his days are numbered and lonely. Tough breaks!

These are both enough to drive any man to breaking point really, wouldn't we all go a little insane if subjected to such tragedies? Wouldn't we all be angry at the world, especially if we've lived a lawful and noble life? Wouldn't we all want to lash out somehow?

Of course we would, but for most of us that wouldn't involve bombing an entire shopping precinct. Most normal people would just kill the wife and be done with it!

I try to convince myself that doing nothing would be a just and reasonable reaction as beer 6 slowly disappears - but I know it's not. Part of me is considering it, because it's the easy way out, it's the path of least resistance. Just make sure no one I know or care about goes shopping that day.

Then just live with it on my conscience for the rest of my life, just like I do with everything else, just add it to the list. Live the rest of my life effectively knowing I let many, many people be brutally murdered on Christmas Eve. Many completely innocent people - many families - many children.

Yeah Right?!? I'm no saint and have made many a questionable decision over the years, but even I can't shy away from this.

I revisit the crumpled corpse of a child crushed under debris and I know that I have to act. I see people dying surrounded by tinsel, baubles and wrapping paper and I know I have to act.

So what do I do? How exactly do you act upon such

information? I need to acquire some semblance of evidence or proof and then approach the police I figure? I need to present them with something on which I can pin my outrageous claims, otherwise I will be laughed out of there.

Suddenly Dex gets to his feet and wanders over to my satchel resting in the corner. Again he has me transfixed as he pushes his snout inside and rummages. No doubt he's onto something. No doubt he will give me the answers.

He's a wise old dog is Dex, a wise old dog of 13 years. Me and him have some kind of natural bond, we can understand each other on some level, so whenever he makes such purposeful moves like this, he always has my full attention.

He can tell I'm wrestling with a massive decision, he knows the burdens I bear. He knows the weights my gift can place on my shoulders, and as I finish the 6$^{th}$ can, he can tell I'm struggling for information.

I say he knows all this but he could just be a dog of course. I'm so lonely I have probably transposed some type of humanistic bond and understanding upon a loyal companion.

I toss the empty can onto the pile. 6 down in half an hour and I'm afraid to stand up too quickly. Steadying myself against a cupboard I gradually get to my feet, my head already spinning and a headache incoming.

I see Dex pull some tissue from my satchel, followed by some gum and some sweets. I think for a moment he may be hungry but I'm too consumed and tipsy to do anything about it for the minute. If there is anything edible in there he is welcome to it. Sod it.

I slump back down into my reading chair and cradle my thumping head in my hands. My head feels like the whole world has taken residence inside it, the whole world feels placed upon my shoulders and all I did was grasp a man's watch.

I hear a faint clatter of keys and suddenly Dex appears in my lap. My Van keys in his mouth. I gaze down at him confused at first, but sensing there is a message here. He forcefully shoves them into my hand as I offer it up and suddenly it all becomes clear. The haze begins to abate and the path reveals itself.

I must hit the road.

I must pursue.

Dex is trying to tell me as much - get in the van and do something. Do something about this for once. Follow this man, stay close enough to him to gather some evidence, but far enough away to keep from danger. I saw where he lives in the visions, it's not local but it's within a couple of hours.

It's pretty much the end of the season, so I have an open calendar. There is literally nothing stopping me doing this and I am obliged to do something. I've been a coward and ignored my visions for so long, but this feels different, this feels purposeful, this feels like a life defining adventure.

If I don't, I will be forever haunted by the twisted mounds of bodies that this man's actions will produce, I will feel partly responsible if I sit back and do nothing.

I will hunt down this man, watch him from afar, wait for him to stockpile fertiliser, wait for him to start abusing prostitutes. I will play detective and gather some semblance of evidence, something tangible to back up my crazy premonitions, then I'll contact the authorities.

I don't intent to intervene directly - I'm a coward - but I can make the professionals do something if I have proof. I can gather some evidence that will make them trail this man themselves; I can give them the nudge they will need to take me seriously.

I smile at Dex and pat him feverishly. I tell him he's done well; he's inspired this lazy bastard once more. I tell him were going on an adventure, were going on a road trip. I tell him we have to do something to save those innocent people and that this is all the kind of exciting drama that a young girl would find irresistible!

    This kind of adventure is just what Alice would love.

# Chapter 12

It's later that day now and I've just taken Alice to a local gig. I dragged her out of work early to catch a hard rocking local covers band.

We drank, we danced, and we had fun.

Were now back at my flat and it's the early hours of the morning. Were in bed and we've just had sex. It was great but felt like the last time. The fair is now closed and the road soon beckons for her and her family.

I'm trying to get round to asking her to come on the road with me, come on this crazy adventure, but for some reason I'm nervous about doing so. I'm slightly scared that she might say no and I'm not sure I could do this alone, Ill end up going slightly mad. I need her company.

I head into the kitchen to grab us some coffee. Dex is sleeping peacefully in the corner, dreaming of bones, of chasing cats, of licking his own ass, his leg flicking intermittently as his mind races. He looks happy.

The kettle is rumbling in front of me and I watch the water bubbling through its glass aperture. The chaos of the boiling water inside brings back visions of rubble, body parts and shrapnel, of a shopping centre crumbling to the ground, of the madness and the pain, of the chaos and disruption.

I spoon out the coffee and see the deep, black pit, torn in the mall floor in the small pile of granules in each cup. I pour out the milk and see the flow of the fire-fighters hose's in the falling liquid. I see blood, sweat and tears in the sugar pot.

I will be haunted by these visions until I can do something about them - until this attack is averted they will forever be in my thoughts I assume. These are not images that are easy to ignore or shut out. I am now a haunted man.

Until now I have never intervened or acted upon my visions with any success, aside from the rescue of Dex of course. I have been very strict and have conditioned myself to be passive, to be apathetic to let things be. To let fate play its hand and let the cards fall where they may.

See it cannot be healthy to start meddling. Where would I be now if I would have intervened all those years ago when I started readings? When I had visions of a young guy falling to his death after a climbing accident?

I made the commitment and decision many years ago that I

simply cannot get involved. Once you start down that road you will never stop, I reasoned. The odd time I have tried, it has spectacularly backfired - so I simply stopped trying.

If I hadn't, I would have been forever explaining, pleading and meddling with people's lives. As much as I would have been helping these people, I've no doubt a lot of them would have taken no notice. They would just be completely confused and upset by my ramblings. I'm not a superhero and I can't be on call to dispense life changing advice every 15 minute sitting, I can't change the future, I can just see it.

I stay passive and merely hint at what is too come. I pass on vague warnings and hope something will seep into their unconscious mind. I try to plant small seedlings that fester and grow inside, hoping the person is swayed into the right course of action when the time comes.

It's really is all I can do. It's all I've ever done. I understand if you hate me for it, but this is my cross to bear and this is my coping mechanism.

So I squeeze the tea bag against the side of the cup and see the contorted body of a young child, crushed under tons of rubble, in its bulging, tea filled sack.

I'm back in the bedroom now.

Alice has dozed off and I perch myself on the edge of the bed next to her, watching the rise and fall of her chest as she breaths peacefully. I place her drink on the bedside table and gently nudge her awake. I need to get this out there and see where I stand, I'm suddenly anxious for her thoughts.

I tell her I've made her a drink, and that I need to talk. She sits up against the backboard and looks at me as if I'm about to deliver some kind of horrifying news. She thinks I'm about the leave her.

She sips at the coffee in silence as I try to muster up some words. Where do I start? Moments pass in awkward silence.

"Well?" she eventually enquires, rubbing her tired eyes.

I tell her I don't know where to start. I tell her I've seen some horrible things and that I need her help. I ask her if she likes adventures, if she fancies a road trip, if she wants to come away with me.

I spit all this out in a flurry of confusion and panic. She stares back at me blankly - the silence is deafening.

"Billy, what the hell are you rambling about?" she has a

look on her face that looks like contempt.

Right at this moment I'm pretty sure she pities me.

I start again. This time I tell her that I've had a premonition, a vision of the future. I tell her that one of my clients will do something unspeakable in the next few months. I tell her I need to trail him and gather some kind of supporting evidence to pass to the authorities. I tell her all this and she still looks like she hates me.

"Billy are you drunk?" scorn adorners her face and in this moment she thinks I'm a crazy old man.

I'm starting to lose my patience.

I tell her that a client of mine will kill hundreds of people on Christmas Eve unless I do something about it.

"Billy, how do you know this?" she is beginning to soften as details emerge.

I tell her that I've had a premonition, a vision that involves a spurned, terminally ill man, getting revenge on his adulterous wife. I tell her that I need to follow this man for a bit. I need to travel south and carry out some surveillance. I need to alert the police, exactly when and how I'm not sure yet - but I need to be close at hand to stop this man. I tell her this will be a fun adventure. I need her to come with me, because I can't do this alone. I love her!

"Billy…." she's smiling at me, a smile so sweet and pure I know I have hit home, "….a road trip sounds like great fun but this also sounds pretty dangerous. Why not just go to the police right now?"

I tell her that they won't listen to me, that I will be accusing an upstanding family man of the biggest terrorist attack in British history. This father of two, this middle manager, this career man, this man with no prior convictions or criminal history (I think?) - is about to snap in extreme fashion.

"Well I guess that makes sense, but how do you know for sure he will do these things?" she inquisitive, but I can feel her intrigue.

Right now she's looking at me like I'm a nutcase.

I tell her I have these visions, these premonitions of the future, that I've had them numerous times over the years. I tell her the story of Dex and claim it was the last time I had such an insight. I am deliberately vague.

Right now she's is looking at me like I'm an idiot.

I continue to plead. I tell her that I don't expect her to understand. I know it all sounds a bit crazy. That it is a lot to ask of her. I also tell her that I need her to come. I tell her that I will sort all this out and be back in a month or so. I'm deliberately misleading about timescale, this could resolves itself quickly, but part of me knows it could take months.

I tell her that we have to do something to save the lives of a lot of innocent people. I tell her this is the adventure of a lifetime. I tell her a lot of things before she finally interrupts.

"Billy, Billy, Calm down babe. I'll come with you don't panic. I could do with a few weeks away from the family anyway." There is excitement in her voice and she reaches over and hugs me.

I had worked myself into such a fevered state whilst explaining all this that I was shaking; her touch is instantly soothing to me. I tell her that it will be exciting and that I am eternally grateful to her. I tell her I love her again and she just laughs nervously.

# Chapter 13

A few days later, I'm outside of the caravan that Alice calls home. I'm propping myself up against the bonnet of my loaded van whilst I wait. Alice is inside the caravan screaming.

The fair season has come to an end for the winter and the mass packing up is underway. The site is almost bare and the 500+ attractions are disappeared slowly for the winter. The families are dispersing to their respective corners of the world. All around are pale patches of grass and dirt trails that weave paths through attractions that are no longer there. Numerous potholes, ditches and rubbish piles also blight the environment after such an event.

Alice is delivering the news to her macho brothers that she's going away for a bit. Tempers are frayed and I'm sipping a beer to try and calm my nerves. My small van is loaded with essentials and Dex has taken root behind the driver's seat. He is excited and raring to go and so am I.

We have camping provisions and intend to pitch up along the coast as we head south. We have a good few hundred miles to cover first so for a while it will be just like a camping holiday. The gypsy van is in lockup for the winter and I'm well stocked with cash and provisions.

We will be on our way as soon as the screaming stops.

Inside the caravan, this will be happening; Alice will be telling them she is coming with me and that there is nothing they can do to stop her; they will tell her that there is no chance she is wandering off with *that* weirdo (I.e. me); she will tell them she is a grown woman who can do whatever she wants and that there is nothing they can do to stop her; they will tell her that I am a waste of time and a loser and that she is better off without me; she will tell them to go to hell and that it is none of their business who she spends her time with.

The thing about Alice is that she is an incredibly strong minded young lady. She will do as she pleases and there is no amount of threats or pleading her brothers can dish out that will change that.

They are just too stupid to realise that the best way to deal with this is to let her go. Stop being so overbearing and just let her get it out of her system, let her make the mistakes that growing up are designed for. Let her hang around with me until she gets bored and moves on. Because she will get bored eventually - I know this and she knows this.

As much as it hurts I know we won't be together forever - there is no happy ending here. She's a young girl who's rebelling against strict parental figures by fucking the local weirdo. I'm just here to enjoy the ride while it lasts.

Inside the screaming dies down and I hear Alice opening and slamming cupboards, I think she is packing her suitcase, but can't be too sure. The screaming will probably commence again soon, but for now its momentarily quite.

Outside of the caravan are parked the two hulking great machines the brothers use for their day jobs, two throbbing, umber macho, motorbikes with fully painted fuel tanks. These tanks are proudly and professionally adorned with the Great Britain flag, and complimented with gleaming chrome highlights throughout the bikes.

They are beautiful machines and the brothers do put on a good show I have to admit - it's somewhat of a dying art and they are part of a dying breed - very few people do this anymore. The brothers are everything you would expect of motorcycle showman - loud, brash, macho to the extreme, and fiercely controlling.

Brad is the oldest and has a perfectly groomed set of blond locks. Looking very much the young Di Caprio, he is the pretty one of the pair no doubt. He's also the slightly more reasonable one and the only one of them with any grey matter to call upon. He's only hit me a few times in the past - mainly the times when Chad wasn't around. Brad's the clever one who works behind the scenes and does the accounts, private event organising, marketing and business decisions, he can be ok Brad - but still far too protective of a 25 year old girl.

Chad on the other hand is somewhat of a monster. He is a hulking mass of a man with heavily tattooed arms, neck, hands and torso - Chad has a tattoo of the devil on his neck. Chad has the words DROP and DEAD tattooed across his knuckles. Chad has spent a few years of his life in jail. Chad's bicep's are bigger than my thighs. Chad has hit me numerous times and broken several of my ribs, he also broke my nose once but that's a long story.

Chad is the muscle - Bret is the brains. Between them they form a formidable partnership in everything from family matters, to business, to putting on a show. They are a tour de force and a pair I've grudgingly come to respect over the years.

Alice and I have been on-off for about 5/6 years. If memory serves me right, I think I first got involved with her when she was 19 - at the time I was 29. I got a beating for that.

The brothers are also a good few years older than Alice, only a few years younger than me in fact, so it really doesn't sit well with them that we rekindle our romance every summer. Over the years we've had many a falling out, it was an annual occurrence for a while, but it's gotten to the point now that we just maintain a cool distance. Long past the fisticuffs and the tantrums, we just stay out of each other's way and let things play out calmly.

The news today would really have upset them though - I could be in trouble once more, but I'm not going to hide away from it.


Alice suddenly springs from the caravan door as I let Dex sips at my beer through the open passenger side window. She has her suitcase in her hand and a look of pure anger on her face - no one puts baby in the corner.

She stamps across the grass to us and throws her suitcase

in the back of the van before slumping into the passenger seat without saying a word. I guess this means were ready to go so I down the rest of the can and toss it aside. Moving round to the driver's side I fumble for my keys just in time to see Chad storming from the open caravan door.

   He looks mad.

   He looks like those cartoon bulls when someone waves a red rag at them. He is charging across the grass between us with arms tensed and veins bulging wildly in his neck. He approaches like a coiled spring, ready and willing to explode.

   I might get punched here.

   The key to taking a punch is to roll with it. Weave with the punch and let your body / face be taken in the direction the fist is moving. Don't resist and try to be a hero, you will be hurt even more. Roll with the punch whilst keeping your mouth shut and teeth clasps together. Don't tense up and try and absorb the punch with a stiff neck. Also try to tuck you chin down to your neck to avoid your head swinging too much from the force of the punch. Another strange, but effective strategy is to try and take the punch on the forehead - duck and manoeuvre so the fist strikes the top of your head. This will still hurt, but the hard surface may just damage the attackers hand and unless he's a superhuman - he won't break any of your bones or cause too much damage, punching such a hard, flat bone.

Anyway, as I try to remember all this, I get hit by the full momentum of an 18 stone muscle man as Chad grabs me by the lapels and throws me onto the bonnet of the van.

Chaos erupts inside the van. Dex snarls and barks like a possessed wolf, howling at the inside of the windshield. Alice springs from the van and comes to my aid, desperately pleading with Chad whilst hopelessly grabbing at his mammoth arms, trying hopelessly to pry them off of me.

His face is mere millimetres from mine as he leans over the bonnet above me, his bald head and colourful skin making for quite a sight at such close proximity - I should be concerned, but we've been here a few times before.

There's a lot of bluster to Chad, he likes to throw his weight around but he rarely throws the first punch. Right now words are coming out of his mouth that I have trouble understanding due to the din around me. Just as he draws back his arm to land his first blow, Bret appears behind him and grabs his flailing forearm, dragging his brother aside with the calm, precocious control of a lion tamer.

I think Chad said he would kill me if any harm comes to Alice whilst we're away - at least that's the general gist of his incoherent ramblings, as he continues to rage at me from behind his superior brothers back. I think I knew that anyway, I'm pretty sure he's been waiting for a good excuse to kill me for some time now, so this is no surprise.

Chad skulks off into the background, dismissed to the caravan by Bret, as I gather myself from the bonnet of my van, trying to gather some sort of composure and straighten myself up. I look up to see Bret pointing a straight, authoritative finger at my face.

"You have been warned my friend…" he snarls in a confidant, stern tone, "….next time I won't be stopping him."

With that Bret turns on his heels and disappears as Alice consoles my shaking body.

Turns out I might end up dying for this girl if this carries on.

# Chapter 14

After all the drama, we eventually hit the road.

What did we learn? Nothing! Her brothers are fairly insane and would welcome any excuse to do me serious harm. None of this is news to us, and I'm sure it won't be the last we hear of them during the coming months. They can't let Alice be for too long so I'm sure there will be numerous phone calls.

Anyway, the important thing is, we're on our way - hitting the open road, heading out of the city and south along the west coast of the country. Our man is still some time away from having his breakdown, so I plan to try and relax and enjoy myself before the storm kicks off. I spun this as something of an adventure & holiday to Alice so I'd better try and have some fun before the horrific events break out.

Alice has been virtually silent since we left the site, so I try to break the tension by joking about not getting a black eye this time.

Right now she looks at me like she hates me again.

"You know what my brothers are like, don't start on them again, they're just looking after Me." she is downbeat and upset. Falling out with her brothers does tend to do this too her, so I better treat lightly if I want sex later.

I tell her I know, but not too worry now - we are on our way and we will have endless amounts of fun. She smiles half heatedly and turns up the radio.

Some indie band is singing the lines "there is bad blood here time, to let it lie..."and it feels like a private performance. I decide to shut my mouth before I make it worst and leave her to sulk in silence.


We pitch up at a campsite a couple of hours later. Alice has been sleeping most of the way whilst I listened to the terrible music coming from the radio. My formative years as a budding musician, then a few more as a roadie, give me the right to judge music of course; and the dross on mainstream radio barely qualifies. When did music become a mixture of synthesised noise with a girl screeching over the top? When did mass produced, harmonized, life-less dross become the nation's favourite type of music? Where did all the rock stars go and why where they replaced with talent show wannabes?

Anyway, the quaint campsite I stumbled upon is beautifully positioned high on a field above a typical English cove, allowing us great views out to sea whilst we erect our tent. Such beauty and serenity has finally started to soften Alice's dour mood, she's still sulking, but just not so loudly now.

Down below in the bay the remains of a bright summers day shimmers and glistens off the water's surface. There is a small and sparse beach with a few small fishing boats moored on their sides, resting at an angle on the beach as the tide slowly seeps back in. There is a small refreshment stand and a few deck chairs, but apart from that, it's empty and secluded. Perfectly relaxing, you would have thought picturesque and idyllic maybe, but all Alice can do is moan about the lack of a decent toilet block.

I tell her these are the kind of facilities you expect for £7 a night.

I starting to think she doesn't like camping much — or she could still be sulking — but it's surprising given the fact she is a traveller by nature, and should be used to this sort of thing. Her mood is such that I wander off with Dex and leave her to unload the rest of the supplies, fed up with her scowl and praying that space and time will soften her up.

Much ado later and night has set in. Dex is asleep in the van, the two man tent being a bit too tight for us all, and Alice and I are snuggled tightly into a sleeping bag. As hoped, time has eventually brought her back to her normal self.

"Billy I'm sorry about today, sorry about my brothers, sorry about my foul mood, sorry today hasn't been much fun." she whispers in drowsy tones as she begins to drift off.

I tell her it's ok and that I'm used to her brothers. I tell her you can't blame them really for being upset; I'd be upset my kid sister was running off with some older guy. I tell her I'm just glad she came and that I'd struggle to do this without her.

She is soon asleep in my arms, and part of thinks this would be a great way to die.

# Chapter 15

It's the next morning now and I've left Alice to sleep in, we're in no hurry so I let her rest. I've freed Dex from the van and am taking him for his morning walk.

If you fail to walk your dog sufficiently it will develop a range of bad behaviours and temperament issues. The dog will become bored and lazy, it will become very unhealthy and as a result, unhappy.

The dog will struggle to socialise with other dogs and will develop an aggressive temperament and attitude. An unhealthy and ill animal will not be a good companion or much fun to keep. Some dogs, especially larger breeds, will develop destructive behaviour if not walked sufficiently. This will include the gnawing, biting and destroying of household furniture and items. The dog will become poorly house trained and your home will become a second toilet for the animal in lieu of the outside world.

A dog that is not walked will become unhealthy, and this will produce generally the same effect as it would in a human – you become lazy and unhappy.

I think about all of this whilst Dex evacuates his bowels

on in the middle of a busy pavement and I realise I have not poo bags on me. I am the scourge of the village, the irresponsible tourist as I have no choice but to walk away. I could be subject to a £1000 fine if caught. I can practically hear the tuts and the curtain twitchers now.

   Dex has been my loyal companion for many years now, but a sudden fear grips me as I divert back off the main roads and into some adjacent fields.

   Whilst one the way down earlier he had a strange sniffing bout with Alice. He suddenly rose from his slumber in the back of the van and popped his head between the front seats. Initially I though he was just saying hello, just looking out of the window perhaps. But no, he stretched over to Alice, who was slumped down asleep in her seat, and started sniffing vigorously. I watched intently as he did this, contemplating the message, but after a few moments he simply stopped and returned to his bed.

   Paranoia grips me as I unleash him to roam the field - what if he smelt cancer again? It may seem irrational, but he had the same look in his eyes, the same short sniffing that accompanies his diagnosis. The only difference being, he didn't place his head on her lap or rub against her in any way.

The fact he physically couldn't due to the vehicle now fills me with fear - what if he had smelt the same thing, what if he was trying to tell me this but the physical boundaries prevented him, what if Alice is ill?

What if Dex knows, but just couldn't tell me at the time? What if I'm panicking for no good reason?

I reach into my coat pocket and pull out a small can of beer. It may be 11am, but I need to settle my frayed nerves, the past few days have given me the shakes it would seem. I'm now inventing irrational fears and concerns.

I take a seat on a fallen tree trunk as Dex digs up the ground off in the distance, leaving him to play I try attempt to settle my wandering mind with booze.

A can or two later and he shows up with a huge stick in his mouth, staring at me as if he's just found treasure. This mangled old branch, covered in mud and grime, is apparently the key to happiness. There is nothing in the natural world happier than a dog with a giant stick, or alternately a dog hanging his head from a moving vehicle.

I've never been as happy as Dex is right now with his huge stick, staring up at me like he's won the lottery, his tail wagging wildly. I wonder if I'll ever be that happy, as I wrestle it from him and launch it across the field for him to chase.

Later now and we're back on the road. Dex still has his large stick in the back of the van. The tent is roughly stored in its original bag, the zip not fully closed as these things never go back in the way they came out. And so the routine begins.

The next few days are a blur or campsites, travelling, beaches and dog walking as we savour the last of the British summer. We spend a few days on a variety of beaches in an identikit number of traditional British seaside towns. We swim, we bathe, we skinny dip - one time, on a secluded beach after sunset - we have sex as the tide lapped at our bare feet.

We spent days eating nothing but chips, ice cream, cream teas and fish suppers. We build a few sandcastles, walk along endless beaches of varying quality and send Dex swimming endlessly in the shallow seas. Together we spend probably hundreds of pounds in arcades, endlessly trying to win the array of tacky prizes that fill up those tedious, but strangely addictive, 2 pence machines. I take her on a famous British pier, and we both have time to enjoy the typical fairground atmosphere without having to work it for once.

In one particular harbour town I treat her to scallops and chips from 'The Best Chip Shop in England', and we spent the evening crabbing off the dockside with cheap lines and slimy bait. We have the time of our lives - the British summer holiday in all its glory and more than enough to justify the *stay-cation* trends.

For a while, I was living the dream and forgetting why all this started in the first place. For a while I was the happiest man on the planet.

Then we reached our destination and things started to unravel.

# Chapter 16

How they rip you off at the fair part 2 - Basketball free throw.

Three shots for as many pounds - get one in, win a prize. Simple! Often the friendly stall worker will offer up some kind of 'deal' to entice you to part with extra shiny coins - often 6 shots for a fiver, scaling upwards to as much as 15 shots for a tenner!

Easy right? Bargain right? 15 attempts to get a ball in a hoop and you get a giant, garish, stuffed animal of some description. You gift it to your lady friend, she instantly loves you forever and you have displayed your physical prowess and alpha male status in a passive, impressive manner. That's what you think anyway.

I vary rarely see people conquer this one, but it remains popular and profitable. What you don't know is that despite the hoop being placed at regulation height and distance, often no more or no less than the standard 3 throw line on a standard court, there are several tricks used to stack the odds heavily against you.

Firstly, the ball is often over inflated and cheap.

Cut price balls are used made from cheaper and lighter materials than standard issue balls. Sufficiently lighter to affect the aim of experienced players, but not noticeably enough to cause doubt to the casual punter. Such light and overblown balls will bounce and spring unpredictably and excessively, if you hit the backboard/ring, and be unpredictable when thrown.

Secondly the ring is misshapen.

It's placed at the right height and distance sure, but it will be far from regulation shape. The ring will be slightly undersized and is often slightly compressed and oval in shape - both indistinguishable from a distance but both significantly reducing your chances. Couple a small, deformed ring with an over inflated erratic ball and your chances disappear.

Lastly there will be a springy & erratic backboard.

Forget the carbon fibre backboards of the pros - the fair will use regular old plywood, dressed up with a lick of paint and a red square to look the part. This again, creates excessive bounce and spring should you aim for it when shooting.

So how do you beat it? Truth is you very rarely do. It's a good old money spinner this one because it appeals directly to any macho man strolling past. Every wannabe sports star or budding athlete, every first dater or guy keen to impress. Every man on the planet who seems to think he is a professional athlete in hiding, a superstar whose career was cut short by fate, chance, or a pure lack of desire. The next Michael Jordan who just wasn't spotted by the right talent scout. Additionally of course, every woman seems to be innately impressed or attracted to an athletically skilled individual - must be hard wired in there somewhere? Sports skills = good mating partner.

Your only real chance is to go high and looping with your shots. Avoid the springy backboard at all costs and go for the old up and under. Attempt a high arcing shot that will drop perfectly through the oblong ring on its way down.

It's not easy and it's very rarely achieved, but when it is - the backboard and ring never come into play. This way you at least reduce the effect of the plywood and dodgy ring - you're just left with a terrible ball to handle. Good luck superstar.

# Chapter 17

So we've arrived in our man's town. We're on the trail. The holiday is over, the fun and games have been put on hold and we're in surveillance mode. I need some proof now; the impending doom is playing on my mind once again, and it's time to get busy.

If I don't act people will die. If I fail a legendry terrorist is born. If this doesn't work there will be a massacre at Christmas.

My visions lead us to a leafy and pleasant street. A street lined with affluent semi-detached houses, a street well-kept and maintained to an excellent standard, a street lined with beautiful oaks that skirt the roadside. As we drive down it, several residents are tending to their gardens in the chilled autumnal afternoon.

Immaculate hedgerows line their territories; perfectly pruned flower beds speak of care, attention and affluence. Each garden is a display of expertise, skill and technique - every garden tells you how rich their owners are and that they have many spare hours on hand. Every garden looks like someone cares for it more than anyone cares for you - every garden looks more important than you.

It's very much the picture perfect, middle class neighbourhood you would expect. Phil is doing well for himself it would seem, this much is clear just from the foliage on display.

We cruise slowly down the street, looking for the light blue door of house no.19 that I saw his wife leaving from in my vision. As we roll slowly along, a bright neighbourhood watch poster catches my eye. It plastered to a telegraph pole that skirts the road and I'm driving so slowly that we have time to read it.

NEIGHBOURHOOD WATCH AREA

Sailsbury Avenue is a recognised neighbourhood watch area

Please report to Phillip Green of No. 23 to sign up or report concerns.


That's our man I tell Alice, pointing at the sign, Mr Phillip Green, would be terrorist, would be mass murdered - also president of the neighbourhood watch scheme for the road.

I quickly accelerate because that kind of stuff will not strengthen my case, and Alice is glaring at me with scepticism laced across her pretty face already.

"Billy is that really the man who will potentially kill everyone? Just that poster makes him sound like something of a saint." she enquired as we drift on down the road.

I tell her that's our guy alright, and that is the man who will blow a hole in the local shopping centre. That's the man who will be pushed well past the brink of human behaviour.

I try to explain to Alice that people can have breakdowns, people can lose their minds when circumstances conspire against them, I tell her life is hard and sometimes brutal, and that most people aren't that far away from doing something horrendous – and that it just takes a certain set of circumstances.

I tell her all of this and she looks back at me vacantly.

Then we reach his house. Outside his wife is tending to a rose bush - she is the typical Stepford wife. She is slim and attractive, perfectly presented and modestly beautiful. The kind of women you would expect to volunteer at the local bake sale, or be a devoted parishioner at the local church. A blue bloused, pearl necklace and pressed trouser wearing, traditional women, who serves her man devotedly and dedicates her life to being the perfect mother. The old fashioned type whose hobbies include flower arranging, baking and plant husbandry. A lady who would tut loudly at any inappropriate language at the dinner table, and be distraught if her little ones smoked or had tattoo's. By all appearances the perfect wife and mother - Phil's done punching well above his weight here.

We cruise past slowly and I whisper to Alice that that's his wife and house. She lurches over me and glares rashly out of the driver side window - Phil's wife notices this. Not surprising given the fact that a strange van is cruising slowly down the road at 15 miles per hour in the middle of the afternoon, she's watching us. I catch her gaze, panic, purposely speed up, and take the next turning off of their road. I pull in when were safely out of sight and try to tell Alice to be more discrete, but she isn't listening.

"You're trying to tell me that that sweet women pruning her roses back there will leave her husband and trigger a massive terrorist attack?", she probes quizzically.

I tell her that marriage and long term relationships are hard, and that sometimes people just want some excitement, sometimes the mundane nature of life is overbearing and that she is already thinking about leaving him. I posit that she may already be having an affair? I tell her that everything is never as perfect as people make it look. I tell her that the kind of life people dream of is never the life they actually want.

"Yeah but that sweet women doesn't look like she could suck the chocolate off a lollypop, let alone have an affair with a toy boy", she rebuffs, clearly sceptical.

I tell her the internet is full of picture perfect women like her who do suck a lot more than lollipops.

Right now she looks at me like I'm a disgusting pervert and a sex addict. She's only half right.

It's later now and Alice is annoying me. We've been waiting in the car for an hour or two, parked somewhat discretely amongst a row of cars a few hundred yards from no.19.

I'm staking out the place from afar, waiting for Phil to return home from work. Trying to hang around for a bit to see if we can get some sort of vibe about their relationship - perhaps later sending out Alice, walking past with Dex to see if she can hear or see anything. Also I'm keen to see if a toy boy shows up to service the wife - thus far there has only been copious gardening and pruning.

Alice is bored and restless. Sometimes I forget she is a young girl full of vim and energy. Sitting around like this isn't fun for anyone, but it requires patience and perseverance. Sadly Alice seems to be lacking both at the minute.

"Billy this is boring. Nothing's happening. Let's come back later", she complains. I tell her that this is what we came here to do; I can't gather any kind of evidence if I'm not around to see it or witness it. I tell her that if we leave, we could miss everything. What if her toy boy is on the way? What if Phil comes home and she leaves him tonight? What if Phil comes home and a huge row breaks out? What if he comes home with a stack of fertiliser already? I tell her all this and she sighs loudly.

Right now I think she feels like Phil's wife - she's contemplating leaving me for a younger guy, someone her own age, who would be at some kind of all-day rave right about now.

An hour or so passes.

Nothing happens.

I send Alice to the local shop for some supplies, we're

both thirsty and hungry, but frankly, I just wanted her out of the way for a bit. The complaints were becoming too much, and me and Dex needed some quite time.

Alice soon returned with drinks and snacks and a trashy magazine to shatter the peace. Hopefully she will be quiet for another hour or so, at least she reads about some sluty Z-list celeb who's just married a football player.

Suddenly after a bit more waiting, Phil pulls up in his people carrier - a bottle green family car with little or no interesting characteristics. Dullness personified. We both suddenly spring into life, and peer intently up the road as our man climbs from his car, gathers his suitcase from the back seat and goes inside.

That's it. Nothing more, nothing less. He came home and promptly went inside - that's what we waited all day to see.

Right now Alice is looking at me like she wants to kill me.

"That's him..?" she asks, pointing a lazy finger up the road, towards no.19, "…that's the terrorist, the demon, the monster? He looks normal!" she continues.

I tell her he is normal, he is average, he is dull - he is

mundane and unspectacular. I ask her what she was expecting - the devil incarnate, a guy with red horns and a tail? Right now Alice is looking at me like I'm a patronising twat. I tell her to take Dex for a walk past the house and see if she can gleam anything at all from the pavement. She half protests as she gathers Dex from the van and wanders off, seemingly enthused by the task.

She re-appears soon after with nothing but a contemptuous look on her face. "They're having spaghetti carbonara for tea", she pouts.

Oh I say.

## Chapter 18

It's the next day now and we've returned to the scene in the early hours of the morning. I intend to follow Phil to his place of work. I need to gather as much information as I can about this man over the coming days; I need to know his routines, his movements, his habits. I need to go where he goes and see what he sees. The more I find out, the better my chances of stopping all of this - the less I find out the higher the chances are that innocent people will die.

We park up down the street and wait for Phil's day to start. He's an office monkey, so I'm assuming he's on a 9-5 clock, and judging by the time he returned home last night, the office is about an hour's commute away. He should be leaving imminently, if I'm right.

Beside me Alice has been complaining some more. She doesn't want to spent the day following this man around, she doesn't want to sit outside an office block and commute to and from a trading estate.

I tell her I don't want to either, but this is what we have to do. If we want to stop people dying, we have to do this. I tell her that this was always the plan, and that she was excited for the adventure before we left.

"Well this isn't the kind of fun I was expecting", she complains as Phil leaves his house and gets into his car.

I want to ask her what the hell she was expecting. Colombo? Sherlock Holmes? Morse? I want to ask her what she actually thought we would be doing once we got here. Raiding this man's home whilst he was out at work for evidence? Kidnapping his wife to stop her leaving him? Apprehending the man, citizen's arrest style, and handing him in at the local station?

I want to ask her all these things, but I can't be bothered to argue and I don't because Phil's on his way, and I must keep up.

We tail him, I think at a discrete distance, for over an hour through red light after red light. It is a drizzly morning and the mood in the car is sour - Alice loudly sighs every 10 minutes or at every long tail back.

She is driving me insane and on the radio some trendy DJ brags about how much better his life is than yours. I start to ask myself why I thought this would be too hard without her. Why couldn't I do this alone?

Right now I'm looking at her like she's a millstone around my neck, a ball and chain around my ankle.

Eventually we hit a stretch of motorway after staring at the back of the same car for 30 minutes. Right here, as we hit the motorway, as Alice and I can barely talk to each other - Phil suddenly takes off! His green people carrying family car literally bolts off along the open tarmac expanse.

I'm visibly shocked, as is Alice, at the sudden urgency involved. "He's seen us, He's seen us - you were too close!" Alice starts yelling as the green blur extends further ahead.

I tell her even if he has noticed us following him, this is rush hour - everyone is going the same way. I tell her that he won't recognise me without my costume and that he has no reason to be suspicious or concerned.

I put my foot down and struggle to catch up with a van full of gear and a large Alsatian to pull.

Ahead in the distance I can see Phil's car weaving in and out of the traffic, switching in and out of lanes and careering forward at highly dangerous speeds, instant ban speeds. He is driving wildly, but for what reason I can't comprehend?

Is he late? Maybe, it's almost 9am so he may be running

late? Whether a middle manager should be that concerned about his time keeping is another question – surely he's on a good salary and should have no need to count his hours and be that slavish to the clock?

"Why is he driving like a getaway driver then if he's not trying to get away from us?" Alice continues, pushing her point enthusiastically. She's not sighing anymore – now she's come alive – she loves the thrill of the chase, and part of me is grateful for the sudden activity.

I tell her that I've no idea. Perhaps something did happen last night and he's an angry and upset man? Perhaps he's suicidal and fancies careering off the motorway instead of blowing himself up in a multi-story?

Minutes pass where Phil's car slowly disappears into the distance. I watch helplessly as his car ducks through tiny gaps, lane hops, and generally annoys everyone he passes. You can hear a chorus of horn blasts as he makes his way through the morning traffic. My van is helpless to keep up and even as I hit 80mph – Phil is still stretching into the distance.

Soon enough we lose him to the horizon. Perhaps he was trying to outrun us? Perhaps he did recognise me and knew I wasn't up to anything good?

I start to panic as I'm stuck on a section of motorway I don't know, and have no idea where I'm heading. Alice starts to complain that I'm a terrible driver and my van is slow, and to be fair both of these are true.

An argument breaks out between us as I jest that it's her weight slowing us down! She screams a lot of words, I don't hear because his car suddenly re-appears in the queue for the next junction. It's a long tail back stretching up the slow lane, and we sail past him in the queue as we occupy the middle lane.

"There he is, There he is…!" shouts Alice, jumping around wildly in her seat - she is really loving this!

It's a long, irritated queue of commuting drivers, but I have no choice but too suddenly swerve in ahead of Phil further up the queue. I take a small gap left as a HGV struggles to pull forward in the queue. I receive loud horn blasts and hand gestures from the lorry driver behind me. I flash my hazards to apologise, but catch him waving a fist furiously in my direction in my wing mirror. I fear another punch on the jaw from the surly, angry driver, but the queue is moving just enough to put him off getting out of his wagon.

We trickle on slowly and I stop looking in my mirrors, so the angry man behind disappears.

Immediately off the junction lies a trading estate and we pull into a lay by and wait by a food vending van whilst Phil catches us up. He exits the junction soon after, and enters the estate without noticing us, his speed still fairly excessive and his driving still aggressive. It's the typical trading estate laden with factories, offices, cars and vehicles, another fast food van and copious amounts of concrete.

He soon pulls into a car park and exits his car calmly, retrieving his briefcase from the back seat before strolling sedately into an adjacent building. He is smartly dressed in a typically corporate suit and has well-polished and shiny leather shoes. He is certainly not a man in a rush - he is calm, sedate and relaxed as her enters work.

"He's weird. I don't like him. What's with the driving? He's not rushing now. He's pretty calm. This man is strange." Alice continues as he disappears in to the building. Confused too, I suggest that maybe he just wanted the rush? Perhaps he was just after a little buzz on a tiresome commute? I say that this could be the first hint of the monster in waiting; this could be the suppressed, rebellious side of this normal man rearing it head? Maybe our guy is a repressed thrill seeker who loves living life on the edge, but a dull marriage and has taken over? Perhaps he's so henpecked that this commute is his only real avenue of freedom? He does look like the type of guy whose wife tells him what to eat, wear, say and do - he looks like the kind of guy who isn't allowed to touch his wife's ass without written consent.

   I suggest that the dormant, sedate part of him cannot dominate permanently - this man likes speed, likes a bit of danger, and enjoys a touch of reckless driving. I posit all this but were still both left scratching our heads at his confusing behaviour.

   Then I ask her if that was fun for her and right now she looks at me with a mixture of thrill and excitement. Now she's staring to enjoy this stalking lark.

# A Reading

*For once, a young lad has wandered in to see me. I suspect he's around 19-20 and out with a gang of friends - he's probably been dared to do this. I had to tell him to leave his beer outside and turn his phone off because he walked in here texting.*

*OMG! TOTES EMOIT! LOLS! #Fortune teller.*

*He can barely sit still and has touched and fidgeted with everything in sight, his eyes have also been darting wildly about the room since entering. I'm fairly positive he's on some kind of chemical substance, but who am I to judge?*

*He's already used the word cool a couple of times - once to describe the chair! What constitutes a cool chair is beyond me, but I get down to business so I can send him on his way as quickly as possible. I hate the vibrancy and energy of young lads like this, such reckless abandon and criminally short attention spans, make them too much for a surely, grumpy git like me. No doubt he has to update his status or upload a picture immediately after, no doubt he wants a selfie with me.*

*I toss around some dice, wave my hands a bit and pretend*

*I'm seeing something in there scattered formation on the tabletop. I then ask him for his watch and he looks at me like I'm a dinosaur.*

*"Aint got no watch dude." he slurs.*

*I sigh and ask for his phone instead.*

*"Me Phone - wat for?" he protests like an accosted school child.*

*I tell him I can see a person's future once I've got a personal possession of theirs to focus on. I can see into the depths of his very soul if he hands it over, and that if he doesn't then he won't get a reading - or a refund either.*

*Grudgingly he hands it over, reminding me it's the very latest model and worth hundreds of pounds, so I better not break it, as he does so.*

*It's at moments like this I'm relived I never had any children. It's at moments like this I realise I'm getting pretty old. It's at moments like this I realise I'm certainly not down with the kids.*

*Clutching his phone, a perfectly designed, expertly made device of communication that now forms the bedrock of a person's life, I am reminded that this thing is probably worth more than my van, and that I would have to complete 20-*

30 readings to have enough money for one of these shiny things.

Where this kid has got the money from I've no idea? I would say that kids these days don't know how lucky they've got it, but that would make me sound like an old man so I won't.

I focus hard and the following things reveal themselves to me.

I see this kid ruining around a football pitch. Evidently he's fairly decent and I recognise the badge and kit as one of the elite teams in the country. I see him score a few goals, I see him celebrate.

Months later I see him wearing an England kit and turning out for the Under 21 version of our national team. This kid has serious talent and it appears he's is not too far away from graduating to the first team, the biggest team in the country.

I see him scoring another goal for the Under 21 England side, I see him celebrate with a bunch of other kids on his team. I see him signing a new contract with his club. He must be something special because this kid will now be paid per week more than most people earn in a year. His weekly pay *cheque is a 5 digit figure! Per week!*

*Flash forward to the summer months and an end of season celebration with his club side. He and a bunch of other kids are drinking excessively in a swanky London nightclub. This kid thinks he's the dogs bollocks, he thinks he untouchable, he thinks he's already made the big time. The sheer arrogance amongst these young athletes is hard to comprehend.*

*Un-surprisingly I see a bevy of artificial, plastic girls hovering around them. These are the type that are tanned all year round, and wear fewer clothes than they do make up. The type of women who are desperate to snare themselves a rich boyfriend, so they don't have to do anything with their lives except spend his money and have his children.*

*I see our star man and a few of his mates taking a gang of girls back to a hotel that evening. I see a raucous party in a large suite, I see coke being snorted in the bathroom. I see our star man with a nosebleed.*

*Then later that evening there's only one girl left in the hotel room with our star man and two of his chief buddies. This girl is heavily drugged, on what I'm not sure, but her eyes are vacant and she is passing in and out of consciousness.*

*I see him and his mates taking turns on this poor girl. She is passed back and forth like a rag doll. I see one of them film some of the proceedings on another swanky phone. I see them all laughing.*

*Eventually they've had enough and leave. They leave the girl battered, bruised and naked on the bed - surrounded by used condoms. I see them stumble off into night.*

*Several months later and our star man and his mates are in the dock. They are up on a rape charge.*

*I see the young girl having a breakdown under cross examination. I see her being accused of lying, of just wanting the attention, of consenting to the group sex session. I see her being humiliated in front of the jury by one of the most expensive lawyers in the country.*

*A few days later and all three of them are let off the hook. Not guilty. No proof that it wasn't consensual and no proof that it was rape. Mr. Lawyer has done his job and receives a large cheque for his trouble. I see our gang celebrate the verdict, celebrate being acquitted of rape. A year or two later and our guy is now a bona-fida superstar footballer. He's repaired his reputation and focused on his game.*

I see that his pay cheques now contain 6 figures per week instead of 5. He is now a millionaire.

Later he plays for England in the world cup finals. He scores a few decisive goals and is hailed as a national hero. His face is branded across every paper and his sponsorships deals rack up even more millions for him.

He is at the top of his game - A world renowned star footballer. His face is on bottles of fizzy pop.

I see he no longer takes drugs, he no longer drinks heavily. I see that he made a severe mistake in his younger years, as most of us would with so much so young, and that he got away with it. He got away with it because he could afford to get away with it - he got away with rape because a lot of people had money and time invested in his future. I see that he was so good and such a promising athlete, that a substantial sum of money was invested in keeping him out of jail. That poor girl was humiliated and shamed because she had the gall to accuse a would-be superstar of rape.

I see all this and I tell our guy that great prosperity is ahead of him, and that he should concentrate on his sport and stay away from the drink and the drugs.

I tell him the world will know his name but not without

*hard work and commitment, reaching the pinnacle of his sport is within him, but he must keep on the right side of the path. I tell him all this in the vain hope he might not rape that poor girl.*

*Then I send him on his way because he's too dumb and ignorant to even listen to what I have to tell him. He's too busy tweeting about it instead.*

## Chapter 19

So now were in a hardware store. A cavernous, huge hardware store with every perceivable DIY material and tool you could ask for. You could build a house with the materials and tools on offer in here.

Phil is shopping with his wife. Alice and I are here also, keeping our distance, trying to get a look at what he's buying, waiting for him to buy fertiliser.

We have a trolley and are pretending to load it with necessities, at least trying to look like were shopping despite the mismatch of items in our trolley. So far we have three different types of wallpaper, a power drill, a tin of paint, a lady garden gnome and an ornate pond statue.

We have been trailing Phil for about an hour, and Alice becoming increasingly bored of picking up random things and moaning at me.

I'm starting to realise why we only normally spend one week a year together. The concentrated period of time would be consumed with sex, drink and good times. No time to be bored and normal. During the mundane practices of everyday life we are far from compatible - if you can call stalking a would-be criminal normal? Part of me feels like I'm babysitting , but part of me also knows I'll never snare a girl like this again, so enjoy it while it lasts.

From afar we can see Phil and his wife stocking up on re-decorating materials. From this I'm attempting to extrapolate where she is in her affair / walking out timeline.

"She's clearly not thinking of leaving him, they just spend 20 minutes arguing about wallpaper. Why would she care if she was leaving him?" Alice reasons, she does have a point I guess?

I try to reason that maybe she's just playing the part, maybe this was all his idea? Maybe she can't decide if she wants out or not and in the meantime will just play the good housewife? Maybe this kind of mundane task will push her over the edge? Shopping for decorating materials is infinitely dull, so maybe this is it - this is the last time they'll shop together?

"Well I thought you saw the future, why haven't you seen this?" she bitches back. We're not getting on particularly well after a few sleepless nights and mundane days.

I tell her I can't see everything and she looks at me like the disappointed lover she is. I tell her that did you know you can make a homemade crossbow with some PVC tubing, strong elastic, and some of the small cam gears in this store?

I tell her this just to annoy her and right now she looks at me with concern and disdain.

We trail at a safe distance as Phil and his wife look around in the garden section outside. Phil's wife definitely has some green fingers and is planning some huge gardening work; she seems to be buying up copious amounts of plant life.

I assume the back garden must be vast or in dire need of updating given the sheer amount of greenery she is picking out. I also assume she hasn't decided to leave yet, mainly because she's still planning large horticultural works. At this point in the proceeding Phil behaves like a normal guy and skulks around after his wife nodding dutifully whilst barely paying attention. If he was any younger he would be browsing the sports news on his phone whilst blindly following her.

Did you know you can make a handheld mini cannon using a deconstructed BBQ lighter, a small pipe, epoxy glue and some bolts? These small cannons will fire ball bearings, and they imitate the air rifles used in the air-softing sport or by marksmen.

In fact a quick look around this place and you will see a mixture of two kinds of couples - behaviour depending greatly on who's wearing the trousers.

If the man's taking the lead you will find them rushing quickly from isle to isle, focusing on the power tools and the hardware; Making quick and unimaginative decisions on aesthetic items, such as wallpaper and paint colours, whilst committing a lot of time and effort to the finer details of their chosen power drill. These men generally have a submissive and placid partner who leaves them alone to work, but insists on coming to the store with their man for, a 'nice day out.'

The other type of couple will be led by the women. These are the strong, decisive and confidant females who like to be assertive and take charge. They have found something for their man to work on, something to occupy him, a task for him to achieve whilst she is out with the girls. These women pick the type of men who will put up with this, and these guys can be seen dutifully following their lady around the store as she makes all the decisions for them. They will spend a lot of time picking out exactly the right shade of paint, agonized endlessly over wallpaper types or garden greenery. These men nod along for a quiet life. They say yes dear a lot. They aren't great at DIY, because they don't really care.

Phil is one of these men.

Alice and I are neither seeing as we aren't actually shopping, and currently hate each other just a little bit.

Did you know you can make a stun grenade with the contents of your kitchen cupboards? All you need is a small pipe or container and some baking soda and vinegar. Alternately you can use citric acid powder and water. These grenades won't cause any harm, but will stun and startle people when thrown, (fire crackers can be inserted to increase the threat level where necessary).

We keep a cool distance as they browse the azaleas. "Why is it so important we see what they buy?" Alice protests whilst fingering a chilli plant. I tell her it's important because within this building you can buy everything you need to make a bomb. It's important because Phil will be here, if not now, then later, buying the stuff he needs to blow up a shopping centre.

I tell her that you can make homemade acid from the contents of your cupboard. Concentrated vinegar is strong enough to burn skin I tell her. In this store you can buy hydrochloric acid, the type that disfigures people horribly if you throw it in their faces.

"You're sick Billy" she responds in a bored and not listening kind of way, whilst wandering off.

Things are getting dull outside in the garden section until suddenly a phone rings. Phil's wife fumbles after it in her handbag. She takes one look at the screen and her face contorts in panic. I can see this because I'm pretending to browse the hanging baskets a few yards from our couple.

She instantly cuts off the phone and shoves it back in her handbag; she is panicked and flustered as Phil enquires about the call. She palms it off as the cold caller we all know it wasn't.

The look on her face, the instant panic, tells me it was someone she didn't want her husband to know about, her face tells me it was her toy boy. Seconds later she tells Phil she is going to the toilet and promptly rushes off, clutching her handbag tightly, and leaving Phil to browse alone, confused and suspicion by his wife's behaviour.

I scoot down an isle or two to find Alice who is browsing the strange collection of garden ornaments. Her face is contorted in confusion at the sight of a 5 foot garden flamingo.

"Who the hell would want that in there garden?" she ponders as I rush up to her. Listen I say, listen - Phil's wife has just taken a highly suspicious phone call, I reckon it was her toy boy I tell her. She's run off to the toilet I tell her, I bet she's calling him back I say.

Right now Alice is looking at me like I'm spouting insanities.

You need to go in there and try to earwig the conversation I tell her. Try and find out who that was, whose she's run off to talk too, find out what the big secret is and why she can't speak in front of her husband.

"Really…?" she protests, "it could be anyone…"

It could I tell her, it could be nothing, it could have been a sales call like she claims - she could actually just need the toilet - but it didn't look like that to me, get in there and find out! It could be the beginning of the end I say!.

I use excited and enthusiastic tones as I say this and it does the job nicely of raising her excitement levels. I make it sound like an important mission that I desperately need her to carry out for me. I manage to fuse ear wigging with espionage and stealth, and after some slight protests, Alice warms to the task.

So I'm now stood outside the toilets with a trolley full of disparate and mismatched items. Alice continued to pick up anything that caught her eye and that now includes another garden gnome, an ornate lamp, and some energy saving light bulbs, a garden gate sign, some expensive door handles and several sample pots of funky coloured paints. Whatever DIY projects we are undertaking needs some serious project management.

I'm waiting anxiously as I have left Phil to wait here for Alice. Part of me thinks I'm starting to get paranoid about all this, but another part is telling me the wheels are now in motion, the butterfly has flapped his wings and the chain of events has begun. I'm anxious to leave Phil unsupervised because he could be figuring out how to make a detonator right now, but I have no choice, this feels important so I just wait patiently.

It feels like decade passes as I stand there trying to calculate the value of everything in our trolley and wait for Alice to return. We've accumulated over £150 worth of tat to adorn our non-existent home and this imaginary palace will be an eclectic mix of masculinity and sickly cuteness.

Did you know to make a petrol bomb all you need is a rag, a lighter, a bottle with a tight neck and, obviously some petrol?

Phil's wife suddenly appears looking composed and relieved and brushes past me on her way back into the store. I watch her disappear into the bathroom suites as Alice appears at my shoulder.

"Caught you looking at her ass" she jokes. What happened, what happened, what happened I probe? Was she on the phone, was she acting suspiciously, was she talking to another man, arranging their next secret rendezvous?

"No Billy, she called her sister. From what I could gleam her sibling is having money troubles and called for help.

Obviously she doesn't work so really she's lending out his money - thus the secrecy." she continues, bored of her own news. I'm also visibly stunned and disappointed by the revelations.

"You know what Billy - I'm starting to think that all this is nonsense. That it's all a waste of time? So far nothing of any note has happened - yet apparently this guy will blow up a mall in a months' time." she says this whilst reaching into my coat and pulling out the van keys.

"I'm waiting in the van with Dex. Hurry up and find some proof", she concludes whilst exiting the store and marching off across the car park.

I'm left stranded in the doorway of the store with my trolley of junk.

Maybe all this is a bit mad? Maybe she's right and I can't trust my visions? Maybe all this is a giant waste of time?


Did you know to make a nail bomb all you need is nails, a two litre bottle, hydrogen peroxide and a hammer?


Leaving Alice to strop alone, I head back out to the garden section just in time to find Phil browsing the fertilisers and soils. In his trolley there are two bags of heavy duty fertiliser. Gathered whilst his wife was absent by the looks of it.

It's far from enough to do the kind of damage I suspect he will, but it's a start; Small acorns and all that. When stuff eventually goes south with his women all he has to do is look in the garage for inspiration. What he has now is the genesis from which the grand plan can spring.

The wheels are in motion, I can feel it, and I know it. Alice can't and thinks I'm insane, but then she was always going too. I'm asking her to believe I have superpowers after all. Nothing tangible has happened yet, but everything I've seen is confirming my suspicions, leading in the right direction.

I've seen enough for the day and grab a single rose plant as I leave the garden section. A little treat for Alice, earn myself some brownie points, maybe get lucky later. I dump the trolley and run, leaving behind its chaotic assembly of items.

I'm at the till point, desperately trying to work the self-serve till. It tells me there is an unexpected item in the baggage area - there are no items in the bagging area. A keen worker appears from nowhere with a clearance card to stop the machine complaining.

"Sorry about this", she continues whilst resetting the machine. She is a kind and friendly looking young lady with long brunette hair and a slightly frumpy frame. Just then a bracelet of hers falls from her wrist and onto the floor.

Ever the gentlemen I retrieve it , and suddenly a vision takes hold.

Chapter 20

A vision in such fashion has never taken hold like this before but right here, at the till point, buying a single red rose, the future or Tracy the shop assistant flashed into view.

I see her out on the town with her friends. She is a big drinker and is having a gay old time. I see her dancing the night away in a terrible club to loud R&B music.

She flirts, she drinks, she socialises. She gets felt up by some guy at the end of the night in a back alley and touches his dick. She says she's not that kind of girl so stops short of fucking him. Instead he gets a hand job.

I see her cleaning her hands with some anti-bacterial hand wash from her purse before sending her mate on his way with a fake number. She knows she will be ashamed of herself in the morning so she gives him 12 digits and tells him to call her. He's not really interested either, so he buys this and wanders off into the night satisfied.

Next morning and Tracy has a huge hangover and a hand that is still sticky for reasons she can't quite remember. She fumbles at a noisy alarm clock before realising she's an hour late for work. She springs from the bed with more gusto and energy than a woman in her current state should.

She stumbles to the floor painfully, hitting her head as she falls, and writhes in pain as the hangover bites. She gradually struggles to her feet before running to the bathroom - she vomits twice into the toilet.

Then, she gets into her car and struggles to put the key in the ignition. She is in no fit state to drive and still some way over the legal limit, but she's about to be late again. She attempts to compose herself before reversing off of the driveway. She fails to compose herself sufficiently because she backs into a lamppost and damages her car. She then cusses excessively before driving off without stopping to check the damage.

She is drowsy but in a state of panic. She fears she may lose her job if she is late again. She is rushing. She is drink driving but it's in the morning so she thinks its ok, she thinks it's the morning so it doesn't count right?

A few miles into her journey she careens around a bend, loses control of her vehicle and crashes head long through a wall. Her car then tumbles down into a small ditch that was concealed by the wall. She blacks out.

She comes too as a hydraulic cutter is piercing the frame of her car. She is being heavily attended too and is currently being closely monitored by a paramedic, she has a neck brace on and a drip in her arm. She also has a tree trunk piercing her torso.

She is fighting for her life.

Flash forward to the ambulance where she is being transported carefully as not to disturb the oak branch sticking in her stomach and out of her back. She is rushed into surgery straight from the ambulance and put into a deep sleep.

On the ward after her surgery, a doctor tells her she is paralysed from the waist down. She leaves the hospital in a wheelchair a few weeks later - a wheel chair she will be forever confined too.

Just then I come too again in the shop as Tracy waves the rose in front of my vacant eyes.

"Sir, Sir, can I have my bracelet please?" she implores. I hand it over in a state of confusion and shock, suddenly realising how this must look to her. Right now I must look like I've seen a ghost in the checkout area. Right now Tracy looks at me like I'm a local homeless guy who's wandered in off the street and never seen a self-serve till point before.

"Are you ok Sir?" she inquires as I gaze at her helplessly.

I'm suddenly desperate to tell her and warn her of what is to come, but am speechless from the shock premonitions. I swallow hard before blurting out that she shouldn't drive after a night of hard partying. Don't drive to work tomorrow - get the bus I tell her. Don't risk your health I yell, then I run out of the store.

I leave Tracy as confused and shocked as I was moments before, as I trail back to the car. I ponder briefly as I cross the car park, why I felt so compelled to tell her? Why am I suddenly interfering after all these years of inactivity?

Perhaps I'm a changed man who enjoys the power, responsibility or authority? Perhaps I like scaring random people as they try to work? Or I do actually care about Tracy and her impending accident? Perhaps all this is true, but maybe this whole Phil thing is making me feel helpless and insignificant, and I just want to make a difference whilst I still can?

## Chapter 21

It's the next morning now and I'm rudely awoken by a harsh and loud synthesised pop song. It's coming from Alice's phone.

We've been staying at a local campsite just outside the city whilst we carryout surveillance and in terms of facilities - it's little more than a rural field. There is a toilet shack and a shower block, but that's about it. It's as basic as a campsite can be, and still get away with calling itself a campsite.

Alice has not been enjoying it, as the days pass she is becoming more and more uncomfortable and irritated. She may have spent years as a traveller, and most of her formative years camping and travelling, but she's accustomed to a bit more luxury than is on offer here. She is used to a caravan providing shelter and comfort, she's accustomed to cookers, electricity and heaters - she's not used to sleeping on a roll mat. I'm starting to worry she may not see this trip out, and that she may well bail on me in the coming weeks.

Given its November and we're sleeping in a tent every night with only the basic supplies, I guess you can't blame her too much?

The harsh music fills the tent and pierces the peaceful morning. We've slept in fairly late, but the deafening tinny ring tone is painful to be subjected too first thing in the morning. Alice fumbles around for the offending object. It's nowhere to be seen as she feels around blindly in the sleeping bag, under the pillow, under a bag or two and around the cramped tent. All the while the harsh pop nonsense pierces into my mind and I have an instant headache.

Eventually she finds it and shuts it up by answering.

For a split second sudden peace and tranquillity is restored and the pain dissipates. For a split second I could hear myself think again. For a split second the world was back to normal.

Then someone started shouting down the phone. Then Alice started shouting back and all hell broke loose once again.

It was her brothers, checking up on her on speakerphone, tag teaming her for answers as to her whereabouts and movements. This is how the conversation plays out in the peaceful, autumnal morning on a deserted campsite.

"Alice where the hell are you?",

"I'm still away with Bill as you know."

"Alice it's been about a month or so, why aren't you home yet?",

"I'll come home when I'm good and ready Chad. What's your problem?"

"My problem is little sis, you've ran off with that weirdo and left us to pick up the pieces. There's a lot of shit we need to be doing in the off season you know this."

"Yeah sure I do, but I'll be back before Christmas so just chill ok?"

"No, no – we're not gunna chill Alice. You've ran out on us and left us in the shit here love, Dad's worried sick."

"Hey! We've had this argument - you knew perfectly well where I was going and with whom, so don't start this again please."

"Yeah we knew alright but I can't remember you telling us it would be so long - I seem to remember you claiming it would be a few weeks at the most. Remember that sis? A few weeks you said?"

"Yeah ok maybe I did but I'm not ready to come home yet. I'm having fun so leave me alone. I'll come home when I'm good and ready brother."

"Oh will you, ok, how fucking selfish are you? Right now

were struggling to make ends meet without your extra income and dad needs a lot more care than he used too.",

"Don't you fucking start on me, you two? I'm not in the mood for this…"

"Oh don't start eh - fine little sister, we won't fucking start, but how about next winter we leave you to care for dad, pay the bills and take care of the van whilst we sod off on some jolly?"

"Listen Bret, I don't have to listen to this; enough with the guilt trips. I can do what I want ok. You're not in charge of me, I'm 25 and I'll do what the fuck I want so back off."

"Yeah ok love. Back off shall we? What happens when that fucker abandons you in a field somewhere? What happens when he's sick of entertaining you and wanders off into the sunset with his stupid dog? What then?"

"Blah, blah, blah boys - how many more times do I have to hear this? You've been saying that for years..."

"What happens then is we have to pick up the pieces. We have to come to your rescue don't we? We have to come get you, bring you home, tell you that you're too good for him and you don't need him. That's what will happen. In the meantime dad will make himself sick with worry."

"ENOUGH. Leave me alone. Stop playing the guilt card just because you have to do a bit extra around the van for a while. Let me have my fun. I've earned it."

It continued in that vein for a while, shouting and bawling in the silent winter's morning, before Alice eventually hung up and started to cry whilst I made breakfast on a tiny camping stove.

## Chapter 22

### How to make a fertiliser bomb

Fertiliser is commonly used to help farm crops grow better and plant life to grow greener and healthier. It is a common product found in any local hardware shop and even some large supermarkets. The manufacturing of fertiliser is where the explosive properties are added.

Large manufacturing plants will treat the raw materials to either purify or increase their concentration, changing them into plant-available nutrients. Part of this manufacturing process is to add Ammonium Nitrate. Ammonium Nitrate (AN) is a chemical compound often found in a white granular form and is added to the fertiliser because of it high nitrogen content. Nitrogen promotes and accelerates plant growth, so it is key to a good fertiliser.

AN on its own is a passive and benign material but when mixed with certain hydrocarbons, it can become powerful explosive material - such common hydrocarbons can include oil and fuel. In the explosive industry they commonly use a mixture of AN and oil for controllable explosions, examples of such uses include building demolition and quarry and mine blasting.

Other applications for AN include some solid rocket fuels, triggering airbag deployment, as a heat absorber in instant cold packs and also in survival packs due to the fact it can be ignited with water.

AN is used to make bombs because of its ability to be combine with a number of other volatile materials. Such commonly available substances as diesel, oil and liquid aluminium's can be used to trigger a reaction.

AN is tough to require in its raw form, but its presence in fertiliser makes it readily available to any would be bomber. To purchase AN in its raw form requires a special license and ID and an individual cannot buy more than would be required for personal use. The seller also has to record the purchaser's info and restrict supplies once such an initial purchase has been made.

Some countries around the world have even banned selling AN in its pure form due to the risk of bomb attacks - these countries include Afghanistan, Colombia, Denmark and China and Algeria.

So instead it's much easier for terrorists to buy

fertiliser by the truckload - A powerful explosion can be trigger with less than a tonne of fertiliser.

To make a very crude and small scale fertiliser bomb you just need the following:

Newspaper

Fertiliser

Cotton

Diesel

You take the newspaper and form it into a pouch as large as possible. This pouch will hold the fertiliser and the larger the pouch, the bigger the explosion.

You then take the cotton and soak it in the diesel.

You then place this diesel soaked cotton, onto the top of the fertiliser in the pouch.

You then light the cotton or the newspaper.

This can be done, if you're suicidal, with a lighter at close range. Alternately this can be done at distance with some kind of explosive trigger, a fuse, or it can even triggered by firing at it with a gun!

This bomb, about the size of an unfolded page of a

newspaper, will cause an explosion covering about 500 square feet depending on the amount of fertiliser used and the effectiveness of the trigger. Simply increase each component proportionately to increase the size of the bomb.

An AN fertiliser bomb was once used to blow up a government federal building in 1995, killing 168 people. To do this the attacker used 2,000 kilograms of fertiliser and about 3k worth of motor fuel. This is about the same amount of material that a large commercial transit van can hold.

## Chapter 23

We're in a model shop now.

Phil is here with his son, spending some quality time. Phil's son is a teenager with acne and low hanging trousers, he has headphone draped around his neck and a large baseball cap perched on his head, a long black fringe obstructs his vision somewhat, he's constantly texting and checking his phone. Something tells me that he is here against his will.

They are browsing petrol driven remote controlled cars, perhaps it's the son's birthday or just a mutual hobby? Alice and I are pretending to be interested in the model trains, but we are not at all interested in them.

The shop is full of tragic old men. Men with little or nothing left in their lives, but to play with little scale models of locomotives. I see virtually no one in the store, aside us and Phil's son, with a full head of hair - in fact I'm certain the shop owner has a wig on.

I see two men in the corner discussing the merits of O gauge model trains as opposed to the N gauge range. These are some of some of the key points raised: O gauge models are twice the size of N gauge and thus there is greater detail and realism in the models. They also tend to be of better quality due to the larger size, thus, O gauge tends to be a bit pricier than their smaller counterparts - but then you get what you pay for in the model train game apparently.

If physical space is an issue then N gauge is the range of choice. This seems to be the only thing it has going for it. The vast majority of enthusiasts prefer O gauge.

I've learnt something today and now so have you.

Alice is behind me browsing the doll's house stuff. It's a small section of the shop, but the tiny little furniture and minute china plates seem to have her intrigued her for the moment.

She has been in a tense and pensive mood after the confrontation with her brothers earlier this morning. She seems torn between a rock and a hard place. I think she wants to stay, wants to help me and see out this adventure, but a large part of her is homesick and guilt ridden.

She is a stubborn girl and the fact that they've taken such direct action, demanding she return home, will only strengthen her resolve to stay as long as she pleases. Part of me wants to take her home; part of me wants her to stay. It's tough seeing her dragged thought the ringer by them, but

I guess they're only acting out of concern for her? They're a nasty pair, but they are only trying to look after her I guess?

This is no consolation to Alice as she fingers the tiny plastic food packages in the kitchen of the doll's house. Everywhere I look in this shop the world has been reduced to miniature. Trains, cars, planes, tanks, houses, animals, people, and infrastructure - an entire planet exists in this shop in small form. It's a freakish place.

Leaving Alice to her tiny house, I browse up the isle further and find a tiny human figure flashing her boobs provocatively at me. From what I can tell these little people are used to dress up a train set, provide some scenery, some human life amongst the buildings and tracks. Accompanying the flasher we have the typical tradesman stereotypes - milkmen, policemen, fireman, farmers, butchers, bakers etc. Everything you could possibly want on your train set is here in minute size and expensive fashion.

I'm distracted by the little people, and in such a lackadaisical and relaxed mood, I forget I'm supposed to be discrete, and wander straight into the aisle Phil is occupying with his son! Pointing and gazing at some small model engine inside a glass cabinet a few meters from me, he seems happy and his son seems vaguely interested.

I panic momentarily, but realise it would be even more suspicious now to turn on my heels and leave the aisle, so I meander slowly down and past my target.

It's the weekend and our man is no longer in the cheap business suits of the weekdays. Instead he has plain denim jeans on, cheap brand trainers and a plain white t-shirt. He is still dullness personified even in his own time. In fact he looks a lot duller now than he does in his business attire - right now he looks like an overweight, unemployed slob. I brush past with little or no fuss and leave the end of the isle, getting a lot closer than a sleuth should.

Phil and his son pay little or no attention to me as I pass and wander off. Again, I'm left to ponder if all of this is really necessary? Is this man really the monster I claim him to be? Is he really a murderer in waiting? Part of me really might think, due to the fact we've been watching him for some time with nothing to report, I might have got this completely wrong?

This could all be a waste of time. This all could be some elaborate subconscious ruse I've cooked up to get Alice to come away with me - this could be a master plan of mine to get her away from her brothers?

All of the above could be true, but if it isn't and he actually is what I expect, then I must continue. If there is even the slightest chance left that this man could be capable of extreme violence, then I need to see this through.

I return to Alice who is now captivated by the tiny chandeliers hanging in the doll's house, lighting up the rooms perfectly as if from a luxurious country home.

"Billy…" she whispers as I approach,

"Is that man really a monster because I'm tired and bored? I get that you're trying to do the right thing and I've had a lot of fun but…." she tails off, focusing on a tiny table cloth as she speaks.

My heart starts to sink.

I know what she's trying to tell me - I know she wants to go home and that she has had enough of this. Whether this has come naturally or been trigged by the strong armed tactics of her brothers, I can't be sure, but I know she's slipping away.

I quietly tell her that I must carry on with this, I must see it out, and that the slight chance that what I've seen will become reality, means I've no choice but to pursue this man. I whisper that if we go back now and the attack happens, I will be forever grief stricken and suicidal. I also tell her that I can't do this without her and to just give me a few more days - a week even - and if nothing has happened by next weekend then we will go home.

I tell her all this and I start to realise I'm more desperate to spend time with her than I am to save all those people - that her company means more to me than the actual act of heroism I'm trying to carry out.

Right now she is looking at me with a mixture of pity and fatigue. Right now I think she wants me to blow up in that mall along with everyone else.

We exit the shop, leaving Phil and his son inside browsing the electronics on offer. We have seen noting once again, either this man is an expert at concealing himself, at hiding his true nature - or he really is just a plain average family man with nothing to hide?

I know which side of the fence Alice is on - she no longer believes me, if she ever really did? She is no longer interested in the chase or pursuit of this man - she is now here under duress. Right now if she could drive then she would go home and leave me to my wild ways.

I spend the rest of the day taking her shopping and buying her nice things so she doesn't hate me so vociferously.

## A Reading

There is a geek sat in front of me. A fully fledged, thick rim glasses, socially awkward, live at home with your mother in you 30's type of guy - the collector of vintage video games, the queuing through the night for the latest smart phone release, type of dude. Completely harmless and a nice enough guy, but a geek none the less. In fact he is so awkward and uncomfortable that he is sitting on his hands and struggling to make any consistent form of eye contact with me.

He wears a t-shirt with a superhero on and his wallet has the character from a famous video game on it - he is a fully grown man with a small, tidy beard, yet he wears cartoon underwear no doubt. He is so timid that I'm worried a bad reading may send him into an epileptic shock.

Anyway such is the sheer size of his nerdiness, I'm certain he will notice a couple of my 12 sided die are from a popular fantasy board game, so I avoid using them and flash a few tarot cards around instead. I think he is impressed because these are cards he doesn't actually collect - although something I see in his eyes tells me he might start after this.

I ask for his watch and he asks what for in the quietest voice I've ever heard emanate from a grown adult.
I tell him it's key to get an accurate reading and that I can't predict is future with it - without it I'm blind. He hands it over without further protest, obviously it's a black rubber strapped calculator watch!

I focus hard and I see the following things.

I see our guy attending some kind of coarse, a summer school, and a two week long intensive course on filmmaking. Seems we have a budding Spielberg in our midst. I see him excelling behind the camera. I see his directional skills impress an instructor who isn't used to this type of proficiency from a beginner. It seems our guy is a natural at this; It seems he has found his calling.

At the end of the course our guy leaves with a

recommendation and an invitation to study an apprentice type position with the instructor, after the impression he made.

I see him packing up his numerous comic books, computer games and figurines as he leaves his moms bedroom at last. See his apprenticeship isn't local, so he has to move away for the duration of the two year study. I see him visibly panicked at the prospect as he boards a coach and waves goodbye to his mother.

I see our guy pitch up at some run down part of an inner city area. It's rough and our guy is not very comfortable with his new surroundings. I see the fear in his eyes that tells me this may be the farthest he's ever travelled away from home on his own.

I see him unpacking in a dingy studio apartment on the $5th^{th}$ floor of a rundown apartment block. It's noisy and from his window he can see a hooker plying her trade down on the corner below.

I see him shed a tear later that night as he tries to sleep on his rickety single bed, complete with stained mattress, and accompanied by various noises outside the window.

Flash forward a year or so and our guy is behind the

camera on some set. It's the set of some terrible daytime soap opera and our guy has his first director's gig.

He is directing a love scene between two bland characters and his is bored of the subject matter, yet enthralled by his job. He is in his element.

A few takes go by, but our guy is not happy with his lead actor, he is lazily spewing his lines with little or no conviction. A few more takes go by before our guy says something to this unconvincing star, asks this professional actor to bring some gusto, bring some zest, put something into it - be a star because right now it's flat and not good enough. Our guy is calling the shots - his anxieties long since faded.

I see the next take and it is worse, the actor having taken umbrage for being called out on his performance. Our guy lambastes him out once more - tells him time is running out and that this needs to be right, he's wasting time and money.

At this the actor throws his toys out of his pram - calls for the management, calls for the boss, accuses our guy of not having a clue, of not being good enough to call the shots, of being a clueless apprentice with no right to dictate to a star like him.

Our geek snaps.

He snaps in a way unaccustomed to him before. The shy, timid and nervous version that moved to the big city full of trepidation and fear, has vanished completely.

He explodes on set in front of the assembled cast and crew, calls the actor unprofessional, and tells him he knows nothing about directing and to stick to his day job. Even tells him he's not very good at his day job by the looks of these takes, tells this arrogant actor that he is an embarrassment, is complacent, that if he doesn't put in the hard graft and apply himself then his future will be elsewhere.

He tells this actor that he will not put his name to these scenes unless he raises his game considerably, then the whole production will stop. He tells him, in front of a large assembled crowd, that the entire production crew will be here as long as it takes, through the night if necessary, because his shoddy performance could ruin the episode. He tells him that there will be hundreds of takes if necessary and that this attitude will keep everyone here all night. You can hear pin drop on set as the dust settles on the director's outburst.

Then a few months later our guy watches his episode on TV, content with the performances and the quality of his first recognised effort. He got results from his snotty leading man eventually that day and he learned valuable lessons - he is chuffed with his first directorial effort. He has come of age, found his niche, found his talent.

A few years later, and our guy is on a film set in Hollywood - he has made it to the big time. He's on a huge film set with several famous actors at his disposal and millions of dollars' worth of expensive production around him. It is some kind of superhero movie and our geeky guy is in heaven - the same superhero he wears t-shirts of at present.

A few months later when our guy moves into a large apartment he now calls home. He has moved his mother in and even has a private arcade and cinema in the sprawling mansion.

This summer course changed his life forever. The placid man faded as soon as he got behind the camera, he found his calling and spread his wings far and wide. It's a rare positive story - for once no one ends up dead or depressed.

    I hand him back his plastic watch with a smile. I'm happy for him; Happy to finally have some positives to work off of. I tell him that he must pursue his dreams, spread his wings, I tell him that his future holds more than he can possibly dream off right now.

    I tell him to keep being a grade A nerd, because it will eventually pay off.

# Chapter 24

Right now Alice and I are in separate parts of the local park.

En route, Alice had been irate and annoyed at me for dragging her off again in pursuit of Phil, whom we followed here from his house. She made it perfectly clear that she's pretty fed up with all this and that she doesn't believe what I tell her about Phil.

When we got here, she shouted, I shouted, Dex barked, and we both stormed off in different directions.

So right now, I'm sat beside a small duck pond in this sprawling city park alone. It's a good size and the largest park in the town, It's also big and fancy enough to have a duck pond, tennis courts, playgrounds and a small café.

Big enough for Alice to disappear out of sight with Dex in, giving us both a chance to calm down a little. I'm left here to stew by the water's edge, watching Phil and his son playing with a remote control car some 200 metres away on a patch of tarmac.

It's a brisk but bright winter's afternoon, and the park is relatively bustling. The sound of children playing is accompanied by the click and clack of the small skate park Phil and his son are hovering around. I can hear ducks, bikes, and kids, and the buzz of the tiny petrol engine Phil's currently trying teach his son how to master.

They seem to be having fun and Phil seems genuinely ecstatic at the father and son bonding session taking place, even his surely teenage son is enthralled by the fast and erratic RC car under his command. They seem happy together.

It's actually a beautiful and heart-warming scene and I ponder briefly that this may be the last time Phil has such a feeling? This could be the top of the mountain, the bliss that will make the loneliness even more unbearable? This could be the last time he has fun with his son? This could be the last time his son likes him enough to spend any time with him?

It's a sad moment and the realisation forces me to avert my gaze and stare at a baby duckling as it chases after his parent across the cold pond water, desperately trying to catch it up, before it gets left behind; Scrambling after something that's just out of reach like the rest of us.

I ponder on Alice and her lousy attitude, as I watch this young thing trailing after its parent - am I too old for her?

Can this really work out given the fact were so different and so in-compatible? Do I want it to work out? Do I want a happy marriage with two kids and a semi-detached town house?

Seconds later I hear a yell, a crunch and an angry reaction emanating from Phil and his son across the other side of the water. I get to my feet quickly and gaze across in time to see Phil's son on his knees beside a crumpled heap that seconds before, was the flying, buzzing RC car so lovingly hand built by him and his father.

An older lad, maybe 19-20, lies in a heap in front on the wreckage, his BMX in a crumpled mess under him as he struggles to crawl from the wreckage. Evidently he was racing towards the skate park and didn't see the petrol RC car skating across the tarmac. Evidently as well as Phil can build small cars, he cannot build them to withstand a collision with a fully grown guy on a BMX.

I'm too far away to hear any words, but what I see from across the serene duck pond, is Phil looming large over this prone kid as he lays prostrate on the floor.

I see Phil's son desperately trying to salvage the many crumpled parts from the concrete and glue them back together with his hands. This is as Phil grabs our wrecker by the collars of his t-shirt and pulls him to his feet. This is as Phil throws a full right hook that connects perfectly with this 20 year olds face.

He's sent stammering back and trips over his prone BMX as he goes, dropping to the floor and clutching his face in agony, I see some blood spurt from his mouth as Phil's right hook perfectly connects. I hear the sickening thud from 200 metres away and it forces me to recoil in horror.

Phil then turns calmly away from this guy and kneels at his son's side too try and comfort him. The poor kid slowly gets to his feet, clutching his throbbing face. Then he shouts some stuff at Phil, spits some blood in his direction, and jumps on his BMX and rides off. He shoots of rapidly towards the parks exits, his pride taken the biggest blow as the assemble skate park crowds all turned and watched as the row erupted.

The entire attack has been virtually ignored by Phil's son who hasn't averted his gaze from his disintegrated machine since the collision. Helping his son salvage the wreckage, Phil and his son walk slowly into the distance, cradling the remnants of their bonding, their relationship - the one thing that has bought them joy and togetherness for many months.

They are leaving the park distraught. All of this happened in a matter of seconds and I'm left stunned and shocked at the scene that exploded from the peace. Confused how violence could erupt from serenity in split seconds?

I have seen the dormant monster! At last I realise I have seen the psycho lurking beneath the surface. What grown man punches a young lad in the middle of a busy park? What father does that in the presence of their child? There is a madman just below the surface and he's getting closer and closer to surfacing.

I have seen some proof at last. Even the sheer lack of a reaction from his sons suggested it was a common occurrence; his dad lashing out wasn't even worth his attention. Maybe he does this all the time? Maybe he does this at home?

I sit back down once again as the baby duck finally catches his wandering mother, regretting that Alice wasn't here to witness this as it may have substantiated my claims somewhat. What does all this mean I wonder as I wait for her to return? How violent is this man under the surface, how short is his fuse, how often does he illicit such violence? Has his wife left him recently? Is that why he's suddenly so angry? Or is this just the savage side of his personality that always lies dormant, always lies in wait?

   Sometime later, Alice shows up at my side with Dex, perching sullenly beside me on the bench, barely managing a greeting. She's still angry and I'm in no mood to compromise so I don't mention what I've seen. I'm too confused to try and explain it anyway, and she's still not talking to me properly. So I just pat Dex in silence.

   We skulk back to the campsite later, again in silence, before I eventually apologies like the grovelling child I am. I apologise because I can no longer remember what we were arguing about and I can't compete with her sheer stubbornness.

## Chapter 25

It's the next day now. Once again there is a deafening noise filling the tent and rousing us from our sleep. It's Alice's phone again. It's Alice's brothers again.

Shouting starts to happen when she answers it so I get up and leave the tent - I sense she may want some space and I can't deal with this again. I let Dex out of the van, he's ecstatic to see me. I don't like him sleeping in the back of a van overnight, but I don't have too much choice at the minute, the tents far too cramped for the three of us and it's too cold for him to sleep outside. He's in good spirits and bounds from the back of the van enthusiastically.

I hook up his lead and we head out for a walk. Whilst doing all of this I've overheard Alice say the following things from inside the tent:

"Please don't start again. I'm not in the mood,"

"Brad, he's not kidnapped me, he's not holding me hostage, were having fun and I'm not ready to come home yet."

"Dad is fine, stop bringing him into this,"

"Why can't you just let me do what I want, why is it such a big deal to you? I'm a grown women Chad, and I'll do as I please."

"I appreciate your concern I do, but I'm just travelling around a bit. It's what we've always done. I'm hardly going into space and back. I'm only a couple of hours drive away so please back off."

I wander off with Dex and let the conversation fade behind me, frankly bored of it and struck with déjà vu. This is all getting a little silly now - her brothers are a bit too intense I think? I think they're straying close to obsessive, crossing some kind of boundary with their constant badgering.

Poor Alice is on the verge of a nervous breakdown, stuck between both parties like this. I let Dex off his leash to run across some empty field that I've stumbled into; he's having the time of his life on this trip, even if no one else is.

I think her brothers must be so intense, because they've never really been separated from each other the years. They've spent a couple of decades holed up as a family together in a cramped caravan, travelling across Europe and around numerous countries.

They've had an eventful and exciting life, tinged with moments of tragedy admittedly, but a close and intense life none the less. The downside of that is her brothers can't seem to deal with her leaving their side for more than a few hours, they're just not used to not having her around and they rely on her more than they would like to admit.

Morning dew carpets the field as I crunch across it after Dex. He's digging up something again, probably looking for another huge stick. It's a bright and crisp winter's morning, and a calming and serene morning's walk does a lot to elevate my frayed and taut nerves.

This is until I return to the tent 30 minutes later. I can still hear Alice talking inside. Her voice isn't frantic, loud or angry anymore at least, but she's still talking to her brothers. She's more composed, sedate and a lot calmer than she was when I left. So the conversation must have moved in the right direction.

Although I was away for a while, so who knows what they've been discussing this entire time? Hopefully they're not still harassing her; hopefully they have got the point at last. I listen closer and realise they haven't.

I hear Alice say the following things from outside the tent:

"Look I think we're gunna start heading home in about a

week or so. I think things are winding down here and the moneys getting tight, so I don't think will be much longer,"

"How's Dad doing? Is he really struggling like Chad is claiming?"

"Can I speak to him?"

"I'm not trying to cause any trouble or upset anyone Dad; I just wanted a little adventure. A little trip away for a while is all. Why are they being so funny about it? Can you have a word with them please Dad?"

"I'll be a week at the most I promise but please get them to leave me alone in the meantime. Please Dad, there stressing me out."

"Thanks Daddy, I'll see you soon. Take care."

From outside the tent I think she hung up after that but I can't be sure. I leave her to her thoughts for a while whilst I head off in search of some breakfast. I'll fetch some stuff from the local shop whilst she gathers herself and calms down a bit.

From the sound of it she's got Daddy to intervene and come to her aid, from the sounds of it she wants to go home in a week – from the sounds of it her brothers may have won.

I may have 7 days left to find a solution to all of this. I might just have a week or so left to save hundreds of people.

# Chapter 26

How they rip you off at the fair part 3 - The ring toss.

Hundreds of milk bottles are spread out in front of you, empty and cap less. Your mission is to toss a small plastic ring over the neck of one of these many bottles. It's a simple set up but next too impossible to pull off from your position behind the stall barriers. You'll normally spend £2-£3 on 5 rings.

The carnie will normally demonstrate how easy this is to achieve. They will do this by using a slightly bigger ring than the ones dished out to the punters. Also from the closer and more favourable vantage point they hold inside the stall, they have a much easier shot.

Often to highlight just how easy is, or to prove that the rings are big enough to fit over the bottles, they will drop one straight down over a chosen bottle. Clearly a vertical drop such as this is a sure fire hit and not really proof of anything, but people are still convinced by it though. Trying to replicate that result from a few feet away and at an acute angle is near to impossible.

They also don't tell you that the rings they dish out to customers are just millimetres wider in circumference than the milk bottle you're aiming for - you've literally got a few millimetres to play with. Unsurprisingly, if you compared the rings the carnie uses to the ones he dishes out you'll see a significant difference, not enough for it to be obvious at a distance, but enough to make their shots a lot more successful.

To make matters worse, the rings are fashioned from hard plastic to cause extra bounce and spring once they are thrown.

Very few people win at this one, your odds aren't great and there is very little you can do to combat the tricks, and even the odds.

The best you can do is to lean over the barriers as much as possible to get a closer shot, but really, even that isn't going to do too much to help you. Best to avoid it if truth be told.

Sad thing is that because of the simplicity and ease of the game, a lot of young children get suckered into this one. A lot of toddlers and young babies often have rings foisted upon them by eager parents, because it's the easiest game to play at the fair. Toddlers can have a go with little or no help - none of them have got any chance.

The odd one will drop over, sheer good luck eventually coming good for someone, but they are few and far between. You've got more chance with the basketball game.

# Chapter 27

After breakfast Alice and I took a trip to the local beach to help calm her down, to help relax things and break the tension somewhat. She was upset, mournful and depressed after the mornings phone call, and the mood needed lifting somewhat.

We had fun, we had ice cream and threw pebbles into the cold water, she smiled for a bit and thanked me for taking her on this trip and apologised for her mood swings. Maybe she doesn't hate me so much after all?

Anyway after all that and all the stress that she's been subjected too over the past few days, she decided not to come out with me tonight. She decided to get an early night and stay back at the campsite instead.

I've taken the bus into town, because there's some kind neighbourhood watch meeting at the local pub tonight. Phil is chairing this informal gathering according to the crude and amateur website and various posters doted around the streets.

I've taken the bus so I can drink a lot. Whilst also watching out for our mate of course - make sure he doesn't do anything suspicious or terrorist like at a small meeting with local residents - but mainly just to drink and drown my sorrows.

I realise how ludicrous this sounds, trailing him at such a conservative gathering, but I'm still expecting something to happen with this guy. I'm still expecting these visions to mean something, and I'm glad Alice has decided to stay back at the site; things seem to happen when she's absent! All I really have at the minute is an excessive overreaction to someone damaging his kids' toy car, but it's a sign and I've got to trust my gift and persevere.

Also it's a good excuse to go out drinking alone - my favourite hobby. Anyway, I enter the pub in question, The Stag and Hounds. It's small and cosy with a log fire, and the obligatory smell of stale beer and old men. It's not quite the quintessential old fashioned country pub, no dog prowling around or homemade beer on tap, but touches such as the open fire and large leather backed chairs make it feel homely. There's also a pool table and a TV broadcasting a sports channel to attract the youngsters in the area, but it's mainly a gentlemen's pub. It's fairly welcoming, despite the cold stares from the locals as I enter and take up residence at the end of the bar.

   Off in the corner Phil and his gang are looking serious and uptight, it's a quiet and fairly empty room so I can just about make out the conversations taking place. My arrival goes unnoticed by them, such are the concentration levels.

   One man is currently railing against the street lamps in the area - apparently he's not happy with the fact they turn off at 11pm due to environmental reasons. He thinks they should stay on overnight to deter any would be buglers or attackers.

   See this is the thing about these middle class types - they are constantly terrified that poor people will take their stuff. When they discuss any potential dangers, they are really discussing how they can protect themselves from the poor, the needy, the foreign, or the different colour amongst them. These cosy and content snobs would like nothing better than to ring fence their little communities, and stop anyone whom they don't approve of from entering.

   I wonder as I down my first pint, if poor people have gatherings similar to this in cheap chain pubs up and down the country, discussing just how to destroy the well off in the area? If chav's hold anti-social gathers to discuss just how unruly and disruptive they can be to the neighbourhood?

I virtually down the first pint in one, such is my thirst, so I order a second beer immediately. As I do I catch Phil's eye from across the pub. Fleetingly and by accident, but our eyes meet and something tells me he recognises me. I can't be sure because he quickly diverts back to his agenda - but he definitely clocked me.

A few weeks ago that would have shaken me, but not now, things has dissipated somewhat. I'm now struggling to see Phil as the monster I've had vision about, just an overprotective dad with some pent up anger issues maybe? I'm still here trailing him, just in case I am right, but I'm now struggling to cling to that assertion with any certainty.

Part of me expects nothing else to happen and for us to head home peacefully in a week. Part of me hopes I was wrong all along. Part of me feels a tinge of regret for this mad cap/mundane adventure I dragged Alice on, part of me just can't decide what to think anymore?

I sink another beer whilst Phil and his gang discus's the need to upgrade the CCTV on the local high street. There have been a spate of thefts from the local fruit and veg shop by all accounts. Here on the outskirts of a major city this is a big deal, here in this little hamlet, this cannot go on any longer.

My guess is a local homeless dude has found a good source for some food, but I could be wrong - it could need urgent and dramatic intervention.

I glance over at the table again and I find Phil watching me. Watching me drink alone whilst a women on his table rambles on about the disabled parking outside the bank. I don't think Phil's very strict with his agenda because they've strayed off-piste somewhat.

Perhaps that's why he's staring at me so intently? He's bored of the nonsense this woman is spouting, bored of hearing about the bank need for three disabled spaces instead of two, just in case the three local cripples fancy going to the back at the same time she demands. Ok love.

I turn back to my beer. Down it and order another. I glance back over to the table and Phil is still staring at me. I meet his gaze and I start to feel the tremble and fear return.

I look into his blank eyes, his odd expression, and I

start to see the bodies, the destruction, the carnage return - the unease and shock I felt back in the reading is flooding back in spades.

I can feel his coldness, his instability, I can feel him creeping ever closer to the edge once again, I can feel why I did this all along, I can feel the end of the world coming in this man's eyes.

Sitting here, staring into his soul, pint in one hand - I can feel the terror rise up once again. This is not a drill, this is not a false alarm. I can feel the switch has been flicked once again, like it was in the park, and the monster is back.

The conviction that drove me here, and made me do this, is resurfacing. Phil is narrowing his eyes and cocking his head in a vague, threatening manner at me.

I can feel him interrogating me from across the pub as we stare into each other's eyes. He knows I've been following him. He knows I know something. I can see him rebuilding the timeline in his mind.

The guy in the park.

The man in the model shop.

The couple in the hardware store.

The strange car following me to work.

The strange car parked on my street.

The strange girl staring through my window that night.

Phil knows I've been watching him and I get this gut feeling that he won't be happy about it.

The threat in his eyes tells me I'm in trouble, tells me that I've been foolish and careless in coming here.

I break his gaze suddenly, and rush off to the toilet in panic, palms sweating. Why have I allowed myself to become so careless and brazen? Somewhere along the line I forgot I was supposed to be conspicuous and stealthy, somewhere along the line I just started showing up within eyesight of him like it didn't matter.

I think it matters now. I'm pissing at the urinal and trying to calm myself when Phil comes in and stands beside me.

"Hello friend", he snarls, the devil in his eyes.

# Chapter 28

Some men are uncomfortable at the urinals. It can be anxious and unsettling for some when they have to try and urinate next to a stranger, their dicks a mere foot apart. Some men try to avoid it at all costs, using the cubicles whenever possible. I've heard others say they've stopped mid-stream when some guy unzips next to them, others can't start when they step into the middle of a crowded urinal and have to eventually give up and come back later. Problems at the urinal are more common that most people would think, or admit. I, myself have never suffered in such a way, and once I've started, there's usually no stopping me.

Unless of course you're a would be terrorist whose just confronted me unexpectedly. My stream is broken uncomfortably and I tuck away discreetly as Phil's threatening words break the silence. There are more pressing matters at hand just now.

I neglect to meet his gaze as he glares at me as I back away from the urinal, I cannot muster eye contact or formulate words. I am stammering and struggling to reply to his thinly veil threatening greeting.

"Well…" he continues, zipping up.

I still can't respond and back away further to the sinks behind us. The devil is in the toilet with me and my heart is skipping numerous beats.

I've had my moments of doubt, my concerns that all of this may have been fabricated in my strange and empty mind, I was beginning to believe that I was wrong, and the nightmare I saw that day at the reading was all my own doing. That it wasn't the future, it wasn't real and it wasn't about to happen. Alice's continuous doubts and scepticisms have gone someway to facilitating this, but I had become too lazy and blasé with my task, and now I'm in trouble. Complacency set in back there somewhere and I've been foolish and reckless - so now I'm in trouble - serious trouble.

The look in his eyes and the deadpan chill to his voice tells me the monster inside this placid man and I wont be leaving these toilets in one piece.

"Why have you been following me?" he poses as he appears next to me at the sink, faintly washing his hands.

I desperately scrub my hands next to him without responding, scrubbing so hard that the skin would disintegrate if I kept it up for any length of time. Apparently experts recommend that the correct length of time to wash your hands after using the toilet is a long as it takes to sing 'Happy Birthday to you' twice through - and also that you should dry them for at least 15 seconds with a towel afterwards.

I'm thinking about all of this instead of responding to Phil, who is glaring at the side of my face as I stare into the sink below, his eye burrowing deep into the back of my skull as I ignore him further.

This will make him angry I'm sure of it, but at this moment I don't really know what to say to him?

*See the thing is mate I've been following you because I think you're about to blow up the city mall with a homemade fertiliser bomb, killing you - your estranged wife and hundreds of people. I'm following you because I think you're in the midst of a breakdown that will have huge consequences for the entire country. I'm following you so I can intervene and alert the authorities before you get the chance.*

I can't tell him any of these things so I tell him nothing at all, I just keep washing. After much excruciating silence I finish washing and turn to leave.

I get all of two steps towards the door before I feel a pair of wet hands grab me by the back of the collar, and the next thing I know I'm being hurled into a toilet cubicle.

I bounce face first off the wall, my left knee ricocheting hard off of the toilet basin as I go. I tumble over on top of the toilet itself, clinging onto its rim like a desperate drunk about to vomit. Stunned and terrified, and thinking how lightly that kid at the park got off.

Behind me Phil appears in the cubicle and locks the door behind him. By luck or design I'm not certain, but it just so happens that it's a disabled cubicle so there's plenty of room for what he has planned.

I try to get to my feet and respond with some words, but nothing comes out and I'm so struck by fear, surprise and pain that I slip and stumble back against the cubicle wall before I can communicate anything, perching on the toilet cistern to break my fall. A right hook strikes me across the side of the face seconds later, and I fall flat onto the hard tiled floor face first.

It's at this point I realise the cleaning regime in this pub isn't the best and the cold, wet liquid that my face has landed in has a stale yellow tint.

I am hauled back up onto my feet by this possessed monster and he slams me back against the cubicle wall and holds me there with both hands. His face is now mere millimetres from mine.

I can smell a mixture or urine and stale beer. It may be the urine on my face or I may have pissed myself - I can't be sure at this moment.

"WHY," Phil screams directly into my face, so close our noses are touching.

It's at this moment that I recognise the absence of a ring on his right engagement finger, a pale white strip of skin in its place.

It's at this point I suddenly start to communicate. I ask him if she's left him yet, if he's been to the doctor, if he's been diagnosed, I ask him how much fertiliser he has in his garage. I slur all this in the gurgled, winded, breathless tone of a man being savagely attacked. Some of this talking un-lodges a tooth and my mouth fills with blood, most of which I spit out as I talk, some of which litters Phil's confused face.

His face, laced with my blood, retorts in anger and confusion at my frantic questioning.

"HAS SHE LEFT ME YET? HAS SHE FUCKING LEFT? OF COURSE SHE FUCKING HAS!" he screams in response, Tossing me across the cubicle floor again as he does so. I slide unopposed through the small puddles and crash hard against the opposing wall, its flimsy plywood construction barely holding on impact.

The next thing I see is Phil's size 6 leather bound loather swinging into my rib cage. I think I hear something crack, but can't be sure because I'm left winded and helpless, writhing in pain in stale urine puddles. Phil grabs me by the hair and pulls my head back, kneeling on the side of my torso he whispers into my left ear.

"She's fucking gone and she will pay.", he says with such menace in his voice, that a chill runs down my spine. Although again, this could just be the piss stained water from the toilet floor.

It's at this point I scream out the word 'CANCER', more blood speckling the floor as I do so.

"How the hell would you know anything about that now? What's your fucking story are you some kind of private investigator? Did she put you up to this?" He continues, striking me across the face with a stray elbow in the process, his overweight frame crushing my chest.

I say the word cancer again because I don't really know what else to say at this point, not with a wild man on my chest and several broken ribs.

"Cancer. CANCER! OF COURSE I'VE GOT CANCER! Why wouldn't a hardworking man who's dedicated his life to providing for his family, get diagnosed days after his wife runs off with a toy boy? Why wouldn't the universe shit on me so badly for no reason?" His voice is a mixture of mania and despair, the kind of mania and despair that will cause a man to do extreme things.

I take a few more punches across the face as Phil vents some more frustration. I think I lose two more teeth during this flurry, but cannot be sure, I also think I black out for a split second because one particular punch bounces my head off the cold floor below.

Right now I think I might be about to die. Right now I'm hoping that Alice will take care of Dex for me and have a long and happy life. Right now I'm wondering why I ever got involved in all this? I should have ignored it all like I have for the past decade or two.

"Listen buddy…" he continues after punching himself out, "I don't know what she's trying to find out, or how much she's paying you, or if she's sucking your dick or what, but you better keep your distance. You better stay away because as mild mannered as I look – I'm not to be messed with."

The look in his eyes as he says these words tells me that here is a man fully intent, and excited, about the carnage he is about to inflict. Here's a man letting the lid off of years of pent up frustrations and resentments.

Here's a man whose life has fallen to pieces and as such – he will makes others experience the same.

Here is the devil incarnate.


I say no more words as he gets to his feet and brushes himself down, straightens himself up and tucks in his shirt. He starts to leave the cubicle and I think I might survive after all. As he opens the door he turns his head and gazes down at me, "Oh and if you go to the police – I'll rape that little slut you've been hanging around with," he says calmly.

With that he turns and leaves the cubicle and the toilets, from my prostrate position on the cubicle floor I hear him stumble out of the toilets into the pub, pronouncing his innocence. Telling someone nearby that he was attacked by 'that stranger' and that he acted in self defence. I hear a voices of consolation and support, I hear them eating out the palm of his hand.

The sounds start to fade as I'm left rooted to the floor. Pain is emanating from numerous points around my body and I'm struggling to maintain any form of consciousness.

Right now I feel like I could have just been hit by a truck.

Right now I feel like my lungs are due to collapse.

Right now I feel like I've seen the devil – and he works in insurance.

## Chapter 29

So it's the morning after the night before. I am outside in a field somewhere, face down on the ground again, but this time, its soggy, cold earth and not ceramic tiles. I am cold, wet, bloodied and bruised, and I feel like death.

I remember the beating and the toilet floor, but after that things are vague. I remember waking to hear the last orders bell ringing in the pub, its ringing rousing me to consciousness on the cold, tiled floor. I remember stumbling to my feet. I remember a rogue wallet catching my eye on the bathroom floor and I remember picking it up.

After that I left the pub via the toilet window. I was in no fit state to walk back through the drunken masses and I wasn't too sure how long I'd been in there. Part of me thought Phil might still be hanging around with his neighbourhood buddies at the bar, but I couldn't be sure.

Instead I climbed out of a small toilet window and crashed into the cold night, the other side. Then I woke up here in this field this morning.

I prop my broken body up against a nearby tree and attempt to gather myself, I'm shivering and chilled to the bone after a night exposed to the biting winter cold.

I think I have the following injuries/health issues:

Two, possibly three, missing teeth.

Cuts to the inside of my gums due to those dislodged teeth.

At least one black eye, maybe two.

Possible broken nose.

Large cut across left cheek.

Suspected broken / cracked rib(s).

My right knee is swollen and bruised.

A huge headache (Possibly a hangover?).

Cuts across the backs of both hands, possibly from defending myself from the barrage.

Possible hypothermia/frostbit.

Aside from all these things I feel good - it's a beautiful morning to be recovering from a savage beating. I fumble in my pockets to see what possession I still have on me; I could easily have been robbed after passing out on a toilet floor for some time. I am surprised to find I still have my wallet, keys and phone - this isn't the rough, low class establishments I'm used to frequenting.

Fumbling further I discover I have two wallets.

The unfamiliar second is a genuine leather bound expensive affair, and is stuffed to the brim with cash. There are a bundle of notes that total about £150. Wow, My lucky day. I should hand it in to the pub of course, this would be the reasonable thing to do, I did retrieve it from the pub toilets after all, I vaguely recall. I think about doing this and then I see the license and I think, fuck it, I'm keeping the cash.

This is Phillip Greens wallet.

He must have dropped it whilst he knelt on my chest, misplaced it when he battered my face. This is his wallet and his cash so fuck him, I'm taking the money and ditching the rest, call it compensation. I sift through to see what else I can find out about our beloved Mr Green, head pounding and my cold breath visible in front of me as I do so.

He has several receipts, some from garden centres and some from various garages - I think he has bought a lot of fuel and fertiliser recently, but can't be sure because there's only vague codes and prices on them, nothing concrete. Card wise he has a standard Visa, a platinum credit card and a bunch of store cards - it's all very mundane.

I toss each card to the ground as I pull them out and empty the rest of the contents onto the damp floor; a family picture drops to the frosty floor at my side.

It's the whole gang - Phil and his wife, posing behind their two kids. The picture must have been taken a few years ago, because Phil has hair and his wife is happy. Also his son looks a lot younger than he did recently. I've not seen the girl in the photo before, so I'm assuming she's away at university or travelling, she's a good few years older than her brother by the looks of it, and must have flow the nest.

They are the picture perfect family - flawless, law abiding citizens who care for the community and respect the elderly. Upstanding community figures with good genes and respectable careers and prospects. This is a long time before the carnage, the chaos, the beatings, the blood and the bodies. This picture is Phil's Mr Jekyll - the complete opposite of his Mr Hyde whose handiwork I am adorned with.

I decide to salvage it from the wet and soggy grass for reasons I'm not quite sure off. Part of me wants this at hand to remind me of the kind of guy I'm dealing with - it could be useful as and when I approach the police - but a larger part of me likes the picture and is quite jealous of the man in it.

   Right there, when he posed for that picture, Phil was living the dream. He was completely happy, the smile is not fake. He has his beautiful wife and adorable kids. He's made it - for a man with only modest dreams, he has hit them spectacularly. He found the love of his life, settled down, and did the kids and marriage thing that everyone thinks they want nowadays.

   Right there - at that moment - our man thinks the rest of his life will play out like some kind of fairytale. He thinks his kids won't end up resenting him, he thinks his wife will never tire of his mundane ways, he thinks they will grow old together and die at each other's side, Romeo and Juliet style.

   The man in this picture thinks the future is bright, thinks the future is taken care of, thinks the hard times are over and it's all sunshine and rainbows from here. This picture is of a naïve man with too much love for a woman who will eventually leave him. This man would lay down his life for this woman at this moment in time. He knows he will do no better, and will spend the rest of his life trying to satisfy her. He will work endless hours and provide more than adequate financial support for her. He will break his back to keep her in a nice home in a great neighbourhood. This woman will never have to work again and will have the luxuries of time and freedom with which to pursue her many hobbies. The man in this picture is the perfect husband and it still wasn't enough.

What hope for the rest of us if this guy can't keep his women happy? How can I possibly satisfy Alice over a long period of time given the fact I can do none of the things Phil has?

My head starts to thump harder at these realisations so I put the notes back in the wallet and slip it back into my pocket, leaving the discarded cards and receipts to the elements as they are no use to me.

Later, I am stumbling back through the town. My phone has died so I cannot call Alice and I intend to return on the bus if I can find the right stop. It was dark last night and in my current state I'm finding it virtually impossible to relocate. Instead I just wander around from street to street, looking like a drunk/tramp/homeless man.

I pass an old lady on the street and she looks at me like I've just stepped out of the trenches. She has a look on her face that tells me you don't see this very often in this peaceful out of town hamlet. It's fairly rare to see a beaten and injured man in broad day light anywhere, so out here it must be particularly alarming.

"Are you ok dear?" She enquires, placing a light and soft hand upon my arm as she speaks.

I am hunched over and holding my left arm across my battered ribs as I walk. I still have dried blood on my face, a patch on my cheek where it's been cut and some patches around my mouth due to the dislodged teeth. My knee is also badly bruised so I am limping somewhat.

Right now, to this sweet old lady, I must look like the living dead - the zombie apocalypse in all its bloody glory. Not what she would expect to see on a Sunday morning trip to the local shop.

I tell her that I'm fine, and that I fell over and spent the night in a ditch, that I'm a drunk so don't feel too sorry for me - and I need to freshen up and does she know of a public toilet anywhere nearby? I also ask her where the bus stop is for the no.19 and she tells me?

"Do you want to come back to mine? We will get you cleaned up and put some bandages on you?" This sweet old dear continues.

I tell her no thanks - I have places to be and that that is the kind of old fashioned humanity that doesn't fit with the modern world. I want to tell her that that kind of random generosity to strangers will get her robbed and exploited, or worse, one of these days. That she should be more careful because not everyone is as nice as me, that the world is full of people who enjoy inflicting pain and misery upon others.

I don't tell her that though because I don't want to ruin her day, instead I stumble on in the vague direction this old dear has pointed, thanking her through bloodied teeth as I go.

Later and found the public toilet. I've cleaned the stains off of my face and am beginning to look like a normal human being again. I still can't walk properly and am still heavily bruised all over, but outwardly I no longer look so 'evil dead' like.

I wonder what Alice must be thinking at this point, whether she's concerned, whether she's noticed, whether she's even awake? I ponder if she has headed out to find me? If she's worried to the extent that she'll try and track me down in the van? After all I did tell her where I was going and promised I'd be back about 12 hours ago, so I hope she's doing something, I hope she cares? I'm momentarily hurt at the thought of her doing nothing then quickly realise that I've got the van keys on me so there's not a lot she can do.

I'm a little more composed and fit for the world again, so I take a drink from the dingy taps to quench my thirst, and head out into the overcast winters day.

I am rejuvenated somewhat and head for the bus, eventually finding the right bus stop after more searching. Whilst waiting I decide to use Phil's money to get me home because - well fuck him, that's why, it's my money now so I reach into my pocket for his wallet.

It's when I touch his wallet that I see the future once again.

# Chapter 30

These are the things I see whilst waiting for the no.19.

I see Phil setting up a bomb.

Before I see him setting up this bomb I see him indulging in a number of lurid sex acts. I see the wheels have come completely off and Phil is running rampant in his wife's absence.

He is in a sex club that is named The Dungeon. The entry price is £50 and for this you get a table and a drink. Also for this you get to fuck the resident sex slave, bound in the centre of the room for all to see. I think she is consenting, but it's hard to tell because she has a gag in her mouth. The assembled punters sit at their tables watching and touching themselves as people take it in turns on this woman.

I suspect that this is a highly illegal, underground, kind of club - the ones you only hear about through a friend of a friend, the type that has a secret knock.

Later I see Phil attend a swinger's party - well probably more of an orgy than a swinger's party. I see Phil having the time of his life as he has sex with at least 6 different women, all with no protection as Phil no longer fears sexually transmitted diseases or more children. The attendees at this gathering are all of a similar age, and ilk to Phil, all highly unattractive and out of shape, all middle aged and overweight, all consenting and enjoying themselves. I start to feel nauseous and thankfully I flash back to the bomb.

I see him using large barrels full of fertiliser and ammonium nitrate. These barrels are half full with fertiliser, a layer of the white stuff on top of this, and then he lines the tops of each one with diesel soaked linen. I see him put the lids on each one as he loads them into the back of a large van, it is clear he has sold his people carrier to fund this new vehicle purchase.

The lids of each barrel have been cropped to allow for the linen fuses to protrude. He buries a good length of each fuse into the barrel to ensure successful detonation and leaves a few feet protruding from the top of each barrel for detonation. Each barrel is connected to a central electrical breaker device that can be remotely operated from a distance, and will spark the sodden fuses into action once activated. I see him test this switch prior to installing and I see the glee on his face after it works perfectly.

As for the detonator, I see him use the modified remote controlled car handset - the one that used to operate his sons destroyed RC car.

Later I see him eating a modest breakfast of bran flakes, topped with chopped banana. I see him putting on his favourite pair of cheap jeans, white trainers, pastel grey t-shirt and his blue Letterman jacket. Inside the pocket of said jacket, he puts his small handheld pistol.

Then he gets into the van. In his hand he has his work briefcase, inside the briefcase is the detonator, and inside the van is a bomb big enough to level a shopping mall.

He drives slowly and steadily towards the mall with a 2 tonne bomb sloshing and rumbling in the back of his van. I see he has a gun in his jacket pocket, a small Smith and Weston type pistol that can be concealed entirely in the palm of a hand. I see he has plenty of bullets for it.

He drives in silence towards the mall on Christmas Eve, whistling merrily to himself as he goes.

I see all this whilst waiting for the no.19.

## Chapter 31

I eventually arrive back at the campsite some time later. I still feel like death warmed up, and that after sleeping in a field during a winter's night, that I'll never feel warm again.

I'm moving a little more freely now and some of the bruising may have reduced judging on peoples more reserved reactions to my appearance - no one is re-coiling in horror like they were this morning.

I walk onto the campsite and wonder what exactly awaits me? Will Alice even be here still, it's almost a full day since I left her here yesterday? She may have thought I abandoned her, and that I disappeared because it all got too much? Right now part of me wished I did do that last night instead of going to that pub.

Where do I start to explain all this? If she's here will she recognise me behind all the wounds, will she be angry, will she be concerned, will she be vengeful? I ponder all this as I cross the field towards our modest tent.

It's Dex that greets me long before Alice does when I get within spotting distance. I can see Alice off across the field; she is sat in the passenger seat of the van with the door open, fiddling with her phone and oblivious to the outside world.

Dex isn't though, I see him lying down outside the tent, his head springs up as I near, bolting from his position, launching like an uncoiling spring upon recognition. I love this dog more than is probably healthy and the sight of his bounding towards me, tongue out and tail wagging, is heat warming. Then I realise I'm in a bit of a fragile state and that an 80 lb male Alsatian leaping at me probably isn't the best thing for me right now.

Off in the distance, behind the bounding dog, I see Alice perk up and gaze across the field at me as Dex nears ever closer - I think I hear her call after him, but it's too late.

He leaps at me with all the enthusiasm you would expect after a prolonged separation, his front paws hitting me hard on the chest and sending me tumbling to the soggy ground. I am winded and gasping for breath as he lands on top of me, his sheer weight and force of impact causing further damage to my potentially cracked ribs, immediately he starts to lick my face and inspect my wounds. It's at once a warm and welcome greeting and physical and brutal assault.

I lay helpless on the ground and let Dex do his thing whilst Alice makes up the ground. I have very little energy left with which to push him off so I lay there helplessly socking up the affection, waiting for a saviour. Soon Alice is stood above us with a look of shock horror on her face. The kind of look the babysitter gets when the killer suddenly comes back to life in those slasher films.

"Billy what the hell has happened to you?" She enquires, kneeling at my side and fighting Dex for some space. I simply say the word Phil and her face drops even further.

I don't explain anything else for a while because Alice sets about doing her thing. She drags me over to the tent and lays me down in it; she fetches some water, some food, some first aid provisions and some towels. I'm cleaned up, plastered, bandaged, kissed, cuddled, licked (by Dex) and generally attended too like a terminally ill patient.

After everything that happened yesterday this comes as a huge relief and right here and right now would be a happy time to die. With Alice doting over my every need and Dex dispensing excessive affection - I would die a happy man if an asteroid hit right now. At some point I fall asleep, exhausted but content.

Later I wake up to find its dark outside and that Alice and Dex are both asleep around me, the tent is bursting at the seams with bodies, animals and medical supplies.

I stare out of the open tent door at my feet and can see the darkness filling the horizon. I start to contemplate where I go from here, what all of this means now and what my next steps should be?

I mull over my options.

Clearly this man is insane - he is a wolf in sheep's clothing and continuing on this path probably isn't good for my health. I'm almost certain, in his current frame of mind, in the midst of his kamikaze breakdown; he will kill me if we are ever stranded in a toilet together again.

I also have no doubts that Alice will be victim to a similar fate, if we keep on pursuing him, and that he will have no hesitation in carrying out his threats should he have the opportunity. I can take the beatings and the attacks – they're probably long overdue anyway, but if any harm comes to Alice over this I'll be forever distraught. I got her into this after all so won't be able to live with myself anymore should he get his hands on her.

I'll be more suicidal than usual.

Maybe I have to get out whilst we've still got our health and our lives? Get out now and save ourselves? Just be totally selfish and ignore what's about to happen, run back home and wait for the headlines.

Could I really do that? Could anyone?

Alice suddenly wakes and startles me momentarily. I tell her thanks for taking care of me and thanks for being here with me. I say that I'll be ok now, just sleep it off and let time heal the worst of it.

"What happened Billy, did you confront him?" She asked whilst resting her head on my chest.

I explain the story to her.

The pub, the toilet, the urinal.

The toilet cubicle, the toilet wall, the toilet floor.

The dislodged teeth, the bruised bones.

The kicks, the punches, the threats.

The wallet, the window, the field.

The cash, the cards, the photo.

Then I tell her I had more visions and I can't see her face, but I feel her roll her eyes. "More visions? Of the attack?" She continues with a weariness and tinge of boredom in her voice.

I give her a quick breakdown of the sex clubs, the orgies and the bomb, and at the end of it she just remains silent.

I don't think she believes in my gift anymore, I think she believes he attacked me because he thinks his ex-wife has put me up to this, and that Phil thinks I'm just a private detective. I think she believes that all this is getting out of hand and this man may well be dangerous, but we shouldn't be getting involved any more.

I believe that is what she thinks, because that's what she tells me. She also tells me it's time to go home and when she does, it's me who remains silent.


It's late now and we haven't really spoken much since. Both of us have been drifting in and out of sleep and generally avoiding the conflict that is due to erupt between us. See I know she wants to go home and I know on one hand she's right, it's the safest thing we could do at this point, but to walk away and let this happen would be a burden I can't live with for the rest of my life. Why can't she see that?

How can I read the headlines, see the news, watch the commemorative ceremony, knowing all along I was the only one who could have stopped this?

"What about the police?" She suddenly blurts, "Is it not time to get them involved?" She continues as I stare at the nights stares outside the tent.

I think that maybe it is, and that it's the easy option, it's the way out of this, but that also I still have no actual proof, nothing for the police to work with. All I have are some crazy premonitions and some bruises. They could call him in on an assault charge, but at this point, a week or so before the attack, he will be bailed and free to carry out the bombing anyway, the threat of a court appearance in a few months won't stop him.

Then he would know I went to the police and he would be after Alice and me, I have no doubt he would carry out his rape threats with gusto and enthusiasm. If he had the chance he'd probably make me watch as he does so. That's the problem - If I go to the police then he comes for Alice. If I go to the police then I have to be certain that he will be indefinitely detained, my evidence must be strong enough to get him instantly remanded and charged. Anything less, and

I'm risking my worthless life and Alice's precious one. No-one gives a shit about my life but I can't put her in such danger.

Until then, there is no way out for me I figure - there is no easy option - I'm in too deep now and I have to see this through - for Alice's safety if nothing else.

I tell Alice all this and she sighs heavily and goes back to sleep. Right now she hates me again. Right now she's is thinking about getting the train home and leaving me to it in the morning.

I eventually fall asleep and dream of a little house in the country. Dex is there. Alice is there. It's the perfect family life - Alice is pregnant and I'm pursuing my artistic endeavours. We are living Phil's dream lifestyle with respectable careers and a burgeoning family life. Our future is bright and we are a picture perfect family in waiting. Then in my dream I see Phil, laughing raucously as he pulls his stocked van up our driveway instead of the mall.

Then in my dream I see my perfect family blown into a million pieces.

## Chapter 32

I dozed off for some time after that, but awake later to an empty tent. Drowsy, aching and concerned, I stumble to my feet and go in search of Alice. I feel strangely lonely and apprehensive that she's not here by my side when I awake - it's a dark and cold night and her absence from the tent is a concern. I remember Phil's chilling threats and am instantly concerned.

I step out of the tent and survey the peaceful campsite, bathed in cool moonlight with a ceiling of stars above. It's crisp and misty and my breath is visible in the frosty winter's air. I see Alice in the front of the van on her phone.

I sigh heavily and stumble over towards her, cradling my ribs and bruised body. She looks concerned and anxious as she exchanges words with whoever may be on the other end of the phone.

The lack of shouting and the time of day, tells me it's not her brothers for once, but it doesn't look like good news despite this. I open the passenger door and slump in next to her, shivering as the cold winters night bites at my delicate body. This is more stress I could be doing without, and even Dex looks at me pensive and confused from the back of the van.

Our trepidation is justified as it becomes instantly clear that she's on the phone to the police. At this minute I'm too tired, bruised and pained, to really care much about this. I should because she could quite easily make me sound like the dangerous lunatic, but I just slump back in the passenger seat and listen instead. Alice and I exchanging the odd glance as she talks, but I make no attempt to intervene, I'll just let this play out I decide let her try it her way.

She says the following things down the phone:

"He's been attacked by this man and he is certain that this attacker will blow up the mall on Christmas Eve."

"He just knows he will, he has seen a vision and hundreds of people will die if you don't stop this man, that's why this man attacked him - because he knows. It was a threat; he was trying to scare us off because he knows were onto him."

"His name is Phil Green I think, he lives in this town and is the neighbourhood watch chairman for Mission Street, that's where he lives, number 19 I think."

I'm listening to all this and thinking that Alice is very naïve - no one is going to act upon the information of a midnight caller claiming to have visions from the future. Telling the police to investigate the neighbourhood watch chairman on this information alone is just a waste of time. That her sweet insistent tone, and good intentions, are ultimately pointless.

"He has a family, but his wife has left him and he has cancer so he's about to go out in a blaze of glory, he's vengeful and angry."

"He has a homemade fertilizer bomb in a transit van and will park on the top level of the mall on Christmas Eve morning trust me."

"After that he enters the mall, kidnaps his wife at gunpoint from a lingerie store and then blows up the place - taking him and his cheating wife with it! YOU HAVE TO BELIEVE ME PLEASE!"

Alice is getting more and more irate as she continues and it becomes clear that they are not taking this call seriously and merely paying lip service to her, no one is listening to this, not really.

"This isn't some prank, this will happen and my friend has just been beating to near death by this man for trying to stop him. You have to do something please," she begs, almost sobbing at the lack of acceptance from the other end of the phone line.

Right now I am only distraught that I get described as merely a friend and nothing more. Right now that hurts more than the copious bruises.

"NO, NO, don't just take notes - do something! People are going to die! DO SOMETHING!" Alice starts to scream as the office on the other end makes it clear that this will just go on file and nothing more. They must get such claims on a daily basis. Everyone's insane nowadays - nowadays everyone's a threat.

"EVERYONE IS GOING TO DIE BECAUSE OF YOU!" she screams and before I can intervene she has thrown her phone at the van windscreen and collapsed into my lap in tears.

Right now this has all been left to me, and me alone - I have to be a superhero now.

## Chapter 33

Here we go again. Alice is on the phone to her brothers again. It's the morning now and I awake to hear her in the midst of another heated conversation outside. I didn't hear her dreadful ring tone this time so perhaps she rang them or I was so out of it I slept right through its awful din? It doesn't particularly matter either way.

I can hear them asking her where she is again, why isn't she home yet? She said just one more week after all, why is she lying? Am I stopping her leaving? Etc, etc, etc. Same old nonsense!

I hear them spout all this and I can't be bothered to listen to it anymore, so I grab the phone from Alice and tell them myself.

I introduce myself and tell whichever one it is that everything is fine, Alice is safe and we're having a good time, I tell them to stop calling every other day and that this constant harassing isn't going to make her rush back to see them. I tell them to stop using their dad as a weapon and to stop making her feel guilty for having a little break, I tell them that we will be back when we please, and that they should just back off.

I scream all this down the phone and Alice has a look on her face like I just killed her cat. Right now Alice looks at me like she wishes she was there to help Phil when he beat me into a pulp.

Seconds after I finish my rant the other end of the phone line simply explodes with rage. So much rage that I simply hold the phone at arm's length whilst a list of expletives and rage emanates from it.

Alice looks at me with hands on hips the whole time, like a disappointed mother. Eventually she snatches the phone back and the following conversation breaks out on speakerphone as she turns her back to me.

"What the fuck Alice - who the hell does that tosser think he is? He thinks he can talk to us like that? That loser, that old man, he thinks he's calling the shots here….?, which brother is screaming this isn't clear, but I'm almost certain they speak in unison anyway so it's not really important, whoever it is speaking so loudly that most of the campsite can hear them.

"Look boys calm down, let's all calm down. Bill's been in a fight so he's a bit fragile at the minute that's all. He's just tired and we woke him up is all. He didn't mean anything by it," she pleads, playing the peacekeeper.

"A fight! A fight! Are you ok? Did you get hurt? What did he do to you? Whose he been fighting?"

"No don't be silly, I wasn't there but a resident took acceptation to his presence in the local pub."

"ALICE THIS MAN IS CLEARLY TROUBLE, THAT'S WHY THE LOCALS ARE BEATING HIM!" I think Chad has the phone now because he struggles to talk in a normal tone and shouts most things like an animal.

"Calm down Chad, it was a one off incident. Don't read too much into it." Alice is desperately trying to calm the situation but she fighting a losing battle.

"DON'T READ TOO MUCH INTO IT! HE'S OUT THERE GETTING PISSED AND BEATEN - HOW IS THAT TAKING CARE OF YOU!" Chad continues,

"Look Chad I'm not having this conversation again. We will be home in a day or two. We're done here now anyway." Alice says all this whilst looking at me and she can see the shock and disappointment in my face at this claim.

"Honest, you will be home in a couple of days? Your leaving today, tomorrow, you're on your way back?"

Alice says yes to this and hangs up the phone, resigned to her fate. She knows she will be going home soon and that a mixture of pressure from her brothers, fears for our safety and sheer homesickness is the cause. However, we didn't agree to this and she knows I won't be going with her, but I think she's going none the less.

I stare at her intently for a few minutes, not sure how to proceed? Perhaps its the situation we're in, her brothers, the shock of yesterday, or the sheer fact we've been away for some time? I cant be sure but regardless, she's had enough now and I can see it in her eyes. Her brothers have given her the excuse she's been looking for, and she's homeward bound now.

"Sorry Billy but I can't do this anymore. I need to go home." She says this and runs into the tent crying.

Later, Alice and I have been arguing for some time.

She wants to go home. Fair enough. So do I, really.

But I can't.

She knows this, but she still wants to go.

She knows that hundreds of people are on the brink of dying if we don't do something about it and she still wants to go home. She knows that there will be a Christmas Eve attack in a few days and that she doesn't care anymore, she knows that little children will die whilst waiting to see Santa Clause and she still doesn't care. I get that it's hard and scary and that all of this is not the adventure she pictured, but how can you not care when the stakes are so high?

I asked her how I'm supposed to live with myself if we go home now and this does happen in a few days' time. I ask her how Billy can live with himself knowing he could/should have done something.

She said she didn't have the answers, but that I'm not a superhero - and if I can't go to the police, then things will just have to play out as they were meant too. Fate wins. Stop trying to be a hero she says.

I plead for a long time with her and I can see it is breaking her apart. I can see that she's had enough of the tent, the field, the cold, the boredom. I can see she's homesick and wants to be home for Christmas. I can see all of this and I do understand, but I'm not going home, I'm not turning my back on this.

Full stop! I'm staying.

I tell her that and she looks at me like I've just dumped her.

Right now Alice has a broken heart.

# Chapter 34

Alice comes to find me some time later. I stormed off with Dex and have been doing laps of the adjacent field for some time, walking off the stress. She approaches across the field, she's cold and wearing one of my spare coats, and has her arms folded tightly across her chest and her head hung in despair.

"Billy, I'm going home. You can stay, but I'm going. My brothers are coming to get me. They will be here tomorrow. I'm sorry. I know you're doing this for all the right reasons, but I'm scared and want to go home." The delivery is so matter of fact and stern that I cannot bring myself to respond. With that she turns and walks away, not wanting, or expecting an answer.

Right now Billy is heartbroken.

# Chapter 35

Alice is leaving so I don't sleep at all that night, I have a strange mixture of feelings about the situation and the conflict is troubling. Plus we're a couple of days away from the attack, so I'm fairly nervous. All in all I just spend the night staring at the blackened roof of the tent and wishing this would all just go away.

On one hand I'm glad she will be out of harm's way, when things turn sour in a few days, nothing pleases me more than knowing, whatever happens, Alice will be safe and sound at home. As much as I want her here with me I can't guarantee her safety so perhaps her being hundreds of miles away is the best thing for everyone? I've no real idea what's going to happen, or how this will play out. So it's a good thing that she will be at the other end of the country at this time. I know I have to do something or I'll never be able to live with myself, but the unpredictability makes it hugely unsafe for her.

Putting all of that to one side, I simply want her here with me. I don't want her to leave me yet, I need her support and her backing precisely, because I've no idea what

I'm doing. I'm venturing into the unknown with possibly life threatening consequences so having her too lean on would mean the world to me. Pretty sure I wouldn't have got this far without her, but she is leaving so I have to deal with it, I have to pull myself together, gather my battered bones, and forge on. This is no time to be needy, this is the time to be a man and finish what I started. I think?

I get up early and take Dex out for his morning walk again. The brisk morning is clearing my groggy mind, and I know all this will be settled in a few days either way so I can get back to normal. I can go back to my shitty life in my shitty little flat with my shitty little career. If I survive that is.

Later that day and I'm sat in the back of the van with Alice and Dex, her brothers are inbound and minutes away.
The van is silent.
I don't know what to say and Alice doesn't know what to say either. We just stare at the floor silently, having awkward conversations about future plans neither us are sure were going to keep. This feels like a break up and even Dex

is depressed. I want her to hurry up and leave so I can have a breakdown, get drunk, and cry.

"Billy…" she says softly, holding my hands in hers, "...thanks for the trip. I've had fun, I really have. It's been special, but all this is too much." Her voice is soft and calm and I detect a hint of relief at the prospect of returning home.

"Please don't bother pursuing that man, he's dangerous and besides I got a feeling everything will be ok, so don't even bother going to the mall. I'm sure it will be fine," she continues softly, desperately trying to convince me to stop when she knows I can't.

She says this and I can see the real reason for her leaving me - she doesn't believe me. She thinks I'm crazy and all this is just a mad dream of mine, she doesn't understand or appreciated my gifts, she just thinks I'm a crazy old man who's got a wild imagination.

I guess you can't blame her - I've still got no actual proof, just some threats, some bruises, some receipts and an angry man whose wife has left him - nothing to convince anyone of the impending doom I have seen, nothing to warn the world with.

I'd like to think that if she actually believed what I was telling her would happen, she would be just as desperate as me too stop it. If she had seen the carnage, the pools of blood, the broken bones and the stacked corpses she wouldn't be walking away like she is. There isn't a person on this plant who could walk away if it was their visions, their premonitions. You can't just turn your back on this, if you believe it, if you've seen it, if you know what I know. I can't blame her for leaving because any other person on the planet would - I'm a wildcard who can't convince anyone of anything - so I guess it's not her fault? I promised a hunt, a fact finding trip and the chance to catch a would-be criminal - all that has happened is that we've argued numerous times, I've been beaten up, and she's been bored. No wonder she's leaving - actually she should have left a long time ago.

I realise this, and am content in knowing that this is all on me and me alone. This is my gift, my burden and my responsibility, so it is fitting that I'm left to finish this alone. I should have never dragged her here with me on this wild goose chase.

Right now I hate myself for being so insecure and fragile

that I had to drag this innocent young girl with me on this misguided adventure.

I kiss Alice on the forehead softly and console her. I tell her that she will be safe back there and that I've had the time of my life. I tell her I don't hate her for leaving and that I'm sorry I ever dragged her here in the first place. I tell her that I'll come to see her as soon as I get back and that I'll bring her a Christmas present, it will be late, but it will be a present none the less. I tell her I'm going to the mall in a couple of days so what do you want?

I tell her this and she smiles at me riley, she knows I'll be at that place on Christmas Eve despite what she says, she knows I'll see this through to the bitter end.

"Earrings, Get me some earrings Billy," she replies coyly as we hear a van pull onto the site and head across the field towards us, we embrace tenderly, both knowing who it is without looking. Her brothers have arrived.

Alice starts to gather her things and silence fills the van.

Soon she will be gone and I will be alone.

She kisses me on the lips and hugs me tightly.

Were both holding back the tears and all that needs to be

said has been said, all the arguments have been played out and we must move on, we have laughed and cried together and now it's time to part.

I HAVE to do this and she HAS to leave. Our paths are splitting temporarily and I think I'm ok with it.

"See you soon Billy, stay out of harm's way you nutcase," are her final words to me as she turns away from me and scrambles out of the van.

I watch her jump out of the back of the van and head over to Dex who's leased up outside and resting. She kneels down at his head and starts to smooth him behind the ears.

"Goodbye Dexy, see you soon," she whispers in his ear. Dex responds by sniffing the air a bit and staring up quizzically at Alice. I'm watching this unfold with a blissful smile on my face, the peaceful and loving interaction of my two favourite companions. The two most loved adored things in my life love each other too, and it's a heart-warming scene.

I'm still thinking this when Dex raises his head up and places it on her lap as she knees on the hard grass. He lets out a bone chilling groan, starts to rub his chin up and down her thighs and looks at me with all the sorrow and regret of a doctor diagnosing terminal illness.

"Oh Dexy your so sweet," she concludes, springing to her feet and disappearing quickly from view.

She does all this before it dawns on me what I've just seen.

She jumps into a van somewhere out of view and leaves before I realise that Dex has smelt something. She is out of my life before I can tell her that she's got cancer. Right now Alice is dying from a terminal illness.

# Chapter 36

How they rip you off at the fair part 4 - The rope ladder.

A devious one this! Seemingly as simple as any other game at the fair - just climbs the ladder and ring the bell at the top. It's no normal ladder obviously. For starters it's set at around 30 degrees and tapers either end into a single point. This single point, top and bottom, means that these ladders freely spin on their axis, pivoting and rotating when weight is applied to them. They are precarious and unstable and regularly throw the overconfident punters to the crash pads below.

There are normally 10 or so rungs from top to bottom and you have to reach the top and ring a bell without falling off or touching the safety mats below to succeed. If you do then the giant gorilla is yours.

This one suckers in all sorts, anyone who fancies themselves to have great balance, really. A lot of young kids eagerly jump on, a lot of macho men who think they can climb anything; a lot of women seem to think they have the grace and fines to get to the top, middle aged family men game for a laugh etc.

Problem is that these things will spin you upside down instantly if you unbalance them, and once upside down it's only a matter of time before gravity takes over.

Sometimes you can swing yourself back up right again, but once you've unbalanced the ladder, it's very difficult to regain stability and reach the top. One false move and it's over very quickly.

This one will never be that easy, but the key is, too completely ignore the rungs of the ladder. Sounds insane right? The problem with using the rungs is that they centre your weight, and any slight deviation from that central equilibrium will send you spinning and falling sideways.

The carnies know this, that's why they normally paint the rungs a nice bright colour opposed to the dull ropes, tempting you onto these unstable planks. Also natural instinct tells you that you must use these rungs, as with any ladder, but this is no normal ladder and the rungs will do nothing but help you to lose balance.

What you have to do is use the side rails for the ladder

to climb with, they're usually made of thick rope. You have to put both hands and both feet on these ropes either side, then have to keep your body low and as close to the ladder as possible, whilst you shimmy your way up the ladder.

However, don't just move both hands and feet up at the same time, the key is to alternate and distribute the weight either side of the ladder at the same time, slowly and carefully you move you right hand and your left foot simultaneously, placing your weight carefully on these points, before moving you left hand and right foot.

You shimmy up the rope sides like this until you reach the top. Equal pressure must be applied to either side of the ladder at the same time as you move. At all times keep your body as close to the ladder as possible to keep your centre of gravity low.

Master this technique and the carnie can do nothing to stop you raiding his oversized stuffed animal collection.

# Chapter 37

It's late now. About 11:20pm and I'm drunk and stumbling towards Phil's street. Me and Dex have been walking for longer than I can recall. We started walking about 8 beers ago. I'm going to Phil's and I'm not sure why?

Maybe I just couldn't stand to sit around in that tent on my own for the rest of the night? It's going to be a lot colder now, there's no 25 year old to snuggle up to after all. Maybe I just wanted to see my new mate Phil, because he's all I can really think about anymore? He's all I can think about, because I can't think about Alice and the cancer for now, I can't deal with that right now because I have to try and save the world first.

I decided to walk so I could drink at the same time and not get arrested for it. It's taken me a lot longer than I anticipated and I may have to find a taxi that will allow dogs, to travel back in.

It's a cold, foggy, deep mid-winter night, and I'm chilled to the bones. Around me are the trinkets and bulbs of Christmas as I walk, giant snowmen, flashing reindeers, singing carollers, fake snow everywhere. Several houses along the way have enough bulbs and ornaments to light up the pavements and make the street lamps redundant, people love to preach the eco card until Christmas where they will happily burn electricity in the name of tradition. Fuck the carbon footprint.

I love Christmas and all its traditions - I love the decorations, the presents, the family time, the magic of it all - but not this year. Christmas will be officially cancelled across the nation if I can't stop this happening tomorrow. The Grinch is about to steal Christmas if I don't stop him.

We're walking briskly and covering a lot of ground so despite the excessive alcohol, I'm not excessively drunk, the top end of tipsy maybe?

Despite all my best efforts not too, as I walk I think of Alice and Dex, and the final goodbye, and whether I'm reading too much into his actions? Maybe he was just sad to see her leave and wasn't offering me a diagnosis at all? Maybe he's as crazy as me and he himself wasn't exactly sure what he smelt? He might just have been confused as to why she was leaving all of a sudden?

Perhaps we are just a pair of idiots who both think they

have access to a vision of the future and special gifts? Maybe he's as delusional as me? Maybe the future has been forever altered by our actions already and all that was to take place no longer will? We branched off somewhere back at the start, a fork in the road was taken and the road we started down no longer exists? Our actions have already altered the future that I thought would happen and now we've venturing into the unknown?

   Phil will no longer blow up the shopping mall, Dex no longer predicts cancer, and I no longer have a gift for premonitions. We came here to change the future and maybe we already have? Don't they say that there are infinite parallel universes? Maybe now we have slipped into a different one where a fertiliser bomb no longer exists? Perhaps the timeline we were on, the one that ended with a terrorist attack, has now diverted to become an altogether different version of the future that's a lot more placid and agreeable?

   Maybe I should stop drinking? Leave all this kind of hypothesising to the clever people eh?

   I'm at Phil's house now, sat outside on the pavement

opposite. There are lights on inside, but only upstairs in a single bedroom, I'm guessing the master due to its size, and that Phil is still up. I'm guessing that he may have a prostitute up there because I can see a lot of shadows dancing off the ceiling, dark and suggestive movements visible through a crack in the curtains. The shadows are fast and fleeting and something's definitely going on in there, something that probably isn't that pleasant.

I'm sat down on the kerbside in the dark of night, watching this ceiling dance, a big Alsatian at my side, a can in my hand. I think I may either end up arrested or beaten to death tonight, and that either way I'm not entirely fussed anymore. I have a large dog with me so at least I have a bit of protection from the devil I seem intent on stalking.

I sit. I drink. I watch.

Nothing happens for a very long time and then a lot happens in a very short time.

I'm just sitting for a while trying to contemplate how to break the news to Alice that she may need to see the doctor, and just how I'm going to explain to her that it was Dex who told me all of this?! Will she even listen, after all the fuss we've had over the whole seeing the future visions already? I'm pretty sure she won't want to hear anymore predictions or premonitions from me, or my dog for a very long time. Perhaps I'll just have to suggest a check-up or something in a subtle and discreet way?

That's if I ever see her again of course. Anyway I'm thinking all this and drinking excessively when Phil's door opens.

A pretty and attractive young lady steps out of the house, Phil stands in the doorway behind with a bunch of cash in one hand, and a dressing gown covering his modesty. He counts through some notes and hands a bunch to the young lady. She is dressed in a long black overcoat that suggests there may be very little underneath it. She also has knee high boots on to complete the look and snatches the cash quickly as Phil offers it.

Then the door shuts and the lady starts walking down the garden towards me. The look in her eyes suggests that she may have left a large part of her soul in that house, the awkwardness of here gait suggests it was physically bruising also.

She exit's the garden, steps past me and Dex and looks at

us like the homeless drunk types we appear. I think I ask her if she had fun in there, but I can't be sure because I'm not entirely sure I can speak coherently at the minute. I may have just made some slurred noises because she's looks down at me like I am the scum of the earth and not fit to lick her shoes. The prostitute, the sex worker, and the women who sells her body to the highest bidder - she looks at me like I'm the scourge of society! It feels good.

Anyway, I guess I must have vocalised something fairly loudly, because Phil's door swings back open immediately after I say these things and he peers down the garden into the darkness where I lurk. He sees me and Dex sat on the pavement outside his garden. I was sat the opposite side of the road earlier, but I must have moved at some point because I'm practically in his garden now.

He immediately strolls out towards us. As he walks I notice that he has a lot less hair than he did last time, perhaps he's started treatment, and perhaps he's just shaving it ahead of the inevitable sloughing?

He stands over me with a mixture of shock and disgust, the moonlight bouncing off his cranium.

"What did I tell you?" He demands, hands on hips in a

dominant manner, dressing gown slightly agape and I'm sure I can see some balls.

I slur some words that were meant to say, 'I know what you're planning tomorrow and I'm going to stop you,' but I'm not sure these words make any sense because he just looks at me confused and irate, before spotting the pile of cans next to me.

"Are you drunk? What the hell do you think you're doing outside my house? I should kill you where you sit you punk." He snarls, finger pointing aggressively in my face. Dex has now become agitated by his threatening demeanour and body language and begins to growl in defence.

I slur out some more words whilst trying to get to my feet. What I meant to do is stand up and confront him. Tell him I know everything and I will not let it happen tomorrow, and that I am onto him and will stop him if it's the last thing I do. I meant to get in his face and let him know I mean business, let him know I'm not going anywhere and that I will raise the alarm as soon as I see him pull his van out of his garage.

I intended to do all this, but as I stand the alcohol takes over and I stumbled backwards and collide with his wheelie bin, Tumbling to the floor atop the contents of the bin that I've now scattered across the pavement and road side.

I'm face down in a pile of Phil's rubbish and have an old banana skin stuck to my face. Other things I see in the rubbish include general food waste, a bottle of used sexual lubricant, numerous decapitated picture of his absent wife, a bottle of expensive perfume that I suspect would have been a Christmas present, various other assorted Christmas decorations, empty bottles of vodka and other such alcoholic beverages, some ladies underwear, some used condoms, a family photo, a pair of flight tickets with India listed as the destination and a passport.

All of this to me looks like Phil is pretty upset with his estranged wife, and bitter about the separation. All this spilt dirty laundry aggravates Phil somewhat, and I know this because he flips me onto my back and crouches over me - he's in my face and grabbing by the scruff of the neck again. I see Dex behind him grabbing and biting at his gown, but Phil simply ignores this.

"I hope you're in the mall tomorrow son. I hope you burn along with the rest of them." He seethes, millimetres from my face at all time. I see the bile in his eyes and the anger raging just beneath the surface in his dead black eyes as he spews this at me. Then with that he spits in my face and starts to leave, kicking Dex aside as he goes.

There is blood on his lower right leg where Dex must have sank his teeth in, and I'm momentarily concerned that it might cause a lot of problems if he reports that. Then I remember what I said and that, at the very least, he will die tomorrow so it's not all lost. OK, so he might take a lot of innocent people with him, but this vile and dangerous man won't be around anymore at least.

Silver linings right? Right?

No.

I see him walk back up his garden and into his house.

I see him shut the door behind him.

At least I know now. I know what he's up to and I need to raise the alarm somehow, I've waited a long time to hear that, to hear that I was right and that I wasn't on a wild goose chase after all. Now, it's my time to act, the time to raise the alarm and to do what I came here for - to intervene. The problem is I can barely walk. The problem is I can barely talk to explain all of this at the moment. I am still just led in a pile of Phil's rubbish whilst curtains twitch in the houses around me. This is a stuffy little neighbourhood and all this commotion could well make the local paper.

I spend the next period of time trying to gather the rubbish from the street and tidy up. All the while spouting nonsense's to Dex that even I don't quite understand, rambling about how he's made a massive mistake and that I'm off to the police station. But first, for some reason, I feel responsible for the mess and put great effort into cleaning it up despite the fact that I can barely stand or co-ordinate my limbs properly.

It's not too long before a cop car pulls up beside me to put me out of my misery. Great I think - they've come to me, saves me going to them. Clearly my presence has disturbed the neighbours and they've immediately called for backup. On what charge I'm not sure, but I guess I could be deemed drunk and disorderly? Perhaps even Phil called them, but I'm not sure even he would be that bold? Surely he doesn't want me in the company of police offices given what I know? Surely that would be too risky.

No. It must have been one of the curtain twitchers.

I'm almost immediately disproved in my theory as one of the officers walks up his garden path to knock on Phil's door whilst the other one bundles me and Dex into the back of the squad car.

I watch from the back seat as Phil and the police man talk on his doorstep. There is a lot of pointing and gesturing and things look calm and amicable from a distance. I see the officer shake his hand and head back down the garden.

It's at this moment I realise what's happened - Phil has called them intentionally. Not because he feels at all threatened by my behaviour, he probably wouldn't bat an eyelid if I slept on that pavement overnight; no he called them for two reasons. One being that if they take me in overnight, as is protocol for drunk and disorderly people - I may not be out in time to do anything about him in the morning. Secondly, he knows I'll run my mouth and try to raise the alarm when in an intoxicated and desperate state. What cop in the world would take the ramblings of an antisocial drunk seriously? He knows that if I mention the bomb plot in this state, then no one will listen and it will discredit anything I try to tell them once I recover.

'Yeah ok, he's going to blow up the mall, of course he is. That's what you kept saying all night when we found you rolling in his rubbish. Also that's what some young lady tried to claim a few days ago - you two trying to set this man up or something?'

I realise all of this and then I realise I can't say a word. Not whilst stinking drunk. They didn't believe Alice when she was sober and coherent - my slurred ramblings have no chance of persuading them. I need to behave and shut my mouth I reason - try to get released tonight or as early as possible tomorrow morning without incident.

I've no idea what time the attack will happen, perhaps even Phil doesn't either, but the longer I'm in a cell the less chance I have of stopping all his.

I'm hoping that he's waiting for the busiest time of the day to strike, maximum casualties assured, so I can't imagine it will be before noon but I can't be sure. I just have to hope and pray I'm around to do something about it.

My drinking has always been a problem, but now it may well have prevented me stopping this, It may well have condemned hundreds of people to death. I think a lot of people will die tomorrow while I'm stuck in a jail cell nursing a hangover. I may have cocked this up big time. Fuck.

## Chapter 38

It's a cold and dark night in the lonely and sparse cell. I passed out immediately after hitting the 6'4" plank of wood that constitutes my bed for the night, the stress and intoxication levels too excessive to do anything but, as soon as I was horizontal. After a few hours the anxiety, the angst, and the impending doom got too me and made sleep impossible.

I'm currently lying on my back on my bed/oversized shelf, staring at the dank ceiling and pondering just how my life came too this? How am I suddenly a menace to society? How did a relaxing trip with my young girlfriend become a lonely and depressing saga that threatens my very life? Are the facilities at the precinct pound adequate for Dex to have a stress free night?

My head is pounding and I've already been sick in the stainless steel, seat-less toilet, in the corner twice since waking, desperately trying to ignore the stains and damp puddles at my knees as I did so.

Some time passes in which I do nothing but think; I think about everything and nothing, about the future and the past.

About my time in Circle Sea, the anonymous metal band I fronted for a few years, and how different my life would be now if that had taken off.

I think about my time travelling Europe with an established metal band as a roadie, and the fun I had on the road with those guys; Even though the job was essentially carrying around other peoples stuff, and setting up for other people to perform - the camaraderie, partying, and adventures, made those years unforgettable.

I think about Casey, my first girlfriend, and how I tried to put my hand up her top behind the bike sheds before getting harshly rejected. How I then moved on to her ugly friend to spite and hurt her - how she then moved onto my friend to do the same, and was infinitely more successful than me.

I think about the time I experimented with drugs at a festival in my late 30's. How I though going to a folk festival, taking various mind altering drugs and not sleeping for 4 days would help me 'find' myself.

About the travelling expedition I took to Australia for similar reasons. This time assuming that what my life was missing was sleeping in noisy hostels with smelly strangers, whilst living out of a backpack and spending countless hours on sweaty cross country busses. People think that travelling will somehow magically transforms their lives - truth is it just puts it on hold. The tedium, numbness, and generally feeling of futility are all still here when you return.

   I think about my parents, long since departed, and I contemplate just what they would think of their only son right now? Would they be proud or ashamed? I'm not sure.

   I am sure though, they would approve of my actions, however foolhardy they may seem, in attempting to do something about the things I've seen. I also know they would have loved Alice and that makes me feel warm and fuzzy inside whilst the chill of night sets in. Jail cells do not have sufficient heating I can tell you.

   I contemplate all of this and a few hours pass, a few more hours towards oblivion/my finest hour. The moon shines bright and full in the night's sky and I watch it through the single, minute window, which sits on the cells outer wall.

   I ponder Neil Armstrong's life achievements and wonder if his footprint is still visible and survived on the moon's surface? Then I remember it was all faked anyway, so it's a pointless argument.

I wonder if the Reptilian Elite really are in charge like that crazy man claims, if global warming really does exist, was it just jet fuel alone that bought down the twin towers, does area 51 exists and if the holocaust actually happen?

Then after all this meaningless reflection and contemplation, I do something I've never thought of before. Something that's never crossed my mind in all the years I've been applying my gifts.

I read my own future.

For reasons I can't really fathom, I just clasp at my watch, focus hard and see various things.

I see myself sat outside the mall waiting for Phil to arrive. I am alone and sat at the entrance to the multi-storey, hidden from view thanks to a large advertising boarding.

Later I see Phil's white transit van scrape into the parking lot under a low hanging barrier and head down into an empty space opposite the entrance. Evidently vans of such a size aren't really supposed to be in the multi-story, but Phil has just about got away with it, the top of the van bearing the marks of the low hanging ceiling.

It's early and he gets a good spot on the top floor of the subterranean car parking lot, the level of the car park that sits directly below the ground floor of the mall.

Sometime later I see myself in the mall itself, watching Phil's wife closely. I see her enter a lingerie shop and then later I see Phil leave with her. She looks distressed and Phil is leading her forcefully by the arm. I tail them through the mall as I contemplate just what to do. Then I see Alice.

Alice is with her brothers; evidently she is in the mall doing some last minute shopping! It seems they must have stayed in town for a night or two before heading home, seeking some last minute Christmas shopping. I feel my heart drop as Alice walks in the opposite direction of Phil and his wife. I see myself struggling to decide what to do, before deciding quickly that I must get Alice out of there. I see myself chasing after her and forgetting Phil, leaving him to his own deadly devices. I see myself picking her life over everyone else's, including mine.

Just then I flash thought the next period of time in a series of vague images that I struggle to make sense of, and that fail to offer real conclusions.

I see the interior of the van, choked full of fertilizer and the make-up of the bomb.

I see Phil and his wife in heated debate inside.

I see a gun, a small pistol in Phil's hand.

I see this gun pointed out the back doors of the van as Phil continues the tussle with his wife.

I see the detonator on the floor of the parking lot.

Flash forward to a vision of me on a concrete floor.

Phil is straddling me, gun in hand, gun in my mouth.

It is unclear what has taken place and weather the bomb is still intact or not. Phil is screaming things at me that I cannot hear whilst I choke desperately on the barrel of his pistol. I see a woman, Phil's wife, running away from the scene over his shoulder as he confronts me.

Then after some time, I see a gun go off and everything goes black.

Then the visions end.

Then I'm back in my cell and I can't sleep anymore because I'm certain I will die tomorrow. I can't sleep anymore because I've just seen my death.

# Chapter 39

So it's the next day now.

It Christmas eve and The Pogues are camped in my head:

*Its Christmas Eve babe,*

*In the drunk tank,*

*An old man said to me,*

*Won't see another one*

I think I might die today and that this song will be the soundtrack. They let me out at early because they didn't want the hassle and there were no charges to press, just a wrap on the knuckles for being a naughty boy and a warning about drunk and disorderly behaviour.

I also retrieved Dex from his kennel and was pretty shocked because the conditions in the dog pound were better than the ones I was subjected too. He is happy and excitable this morning because he missed me last night and because he's had a good night's sleep in his plush doggy basket. Dogs get a plush bed - humans get a hard plank of wood.

I head back to the camp site and fetch my van. I leave the tent and its contents and am destined never to come back. I leave the tent because I can't be bothered with it and it reminds me of Alice. I leave it because it reminds me of good times that may be a thing of the past for me now.

I also leave Dex leashed up outside the tent with a fresh bowl of water and some snacks. Amongst my possessions I leave a note with Alice's contact details and instructions to contact her regarding the dog should anything happen to me - I know she will love and adore him as much as me should I not return.

Before I leave I kneel at his side and try to say goodbye without breaking down. I have people too save, maybe, and if not, I can't let Dex be killed along with everyone else. I have to get Alice out of there before any harm comes too her and if I can't and the worse happens, then at least I'll die knowing Dex is safe and sound miles away.

I cup his head in my hands and push out foreheads together, choking on tears. I hear his heavy breathing and panting, his dog breath and his soggy tongue as it licks at my face. I see his big black eyes, staring deep into my soul - in them I see fear, hope, devotion and contentment.

Call me insane but I think he knows what it is I'm doing, he knows I'm leaving him here for his safety and that I will return should I have the opportunity. He looks at me and he knows I'm doing the right thing.

   He knows that I would never let him come to harm after all of these years together, after I rescued him from neglect, spent a fortune on an operation after he swallowed a rubber ball, spent another fortune on fixing his broken leg after he collided with a car. He's my best friend and he knows somewhere in his canine soul that he cannot help me with this, he knows I'm doing this for his own safety.

   Right now the look on Dex's face says that he loves me and that he thanks me for rescuing him all those years ago. Right now he is looking at me like I saved his life and that its time for me to save others.

   I drag myself away and as I walk to the van, Dex barks a single time behind me. It is his final goodbye and I can barely drive through the tears.

   I head for the town and for the mall.

   As I drive, I realise I still don't know what to do? Despite the excessive visions and premonitions I'm still unsure how all of this will play out? Perhaps I've seen too much to really make any informed decisions? Perhaps this will all play out exactly as I have seen?

If it does I will die today. I have seen the gun, I have seen the killer, I have seen myself chocking on the barrel and the dead eyes of my killer. I've also seen all this of and have no idea if this is post or pre explosion.

What if this is all for nothing? What if I give up my life trying to prevent an attack that plays out after I've died anyway? How ironic. At least if I knew that my actions would have saved a lot of innocent people then I could perhaps die happily? Happy in the knowledge that I made a difference, the Grinch didn't steal Christmas, and that I saved Alice along with hundreds of others.

I would give up my life for a noble cause like that. Why not? I'm a low life alcoholic whose only friend is a Dog, and whose girlfriend is already bored of me - whose going to miss that? I should be glad I can give it all up to save some lives; a lot of people don't get that chance. A lot of people die alone - at least I'll have Phil with me.

If nothing else my main goal now is to get Alice out - whatever happens after that is in fate's hands.

I round a corner and come to the malls entrance.

It's still too early for the stores to be open and the

place is fairly deserted. It's a huge, 100+ store malls that is the epicentre of the towns shopping district, and this will no doubt be one of its busiest days of the year. All around I can see Christmas lights, decorations, copious adverts for all and every type of gift imaginable, and the general commercial splurge that constitutes Christmas nowadays. The weather is suitably seasonal – cold, crisp and bright.

I take my ticket and drop into the car park. It's empty, except for a few employees' vehicles, and I decide not to park on the top floor as Phil will when he arrives. I'm still trying to keep my distance and choose my exact moment to intervene, surprise being my biggest weapon, so parking in plain sight would be stupid.

I head down a few levels and the car park is completely deserted. It's a four level basement car park that holds 300+ cars and it will be full within an hour or so. Last minute gift buyers full of the festive joys and in good spirits, buying gifts to bestow upon their loved ones on the most important day of the year. Spending that bonus on tat that no one really needs or wants, fretting endlessly over that one special piece of junk for a loved one, purchasing yet another toy for that spoilt little brat - all in the name of Christmas, all in the name of love and togetherness; All about to be blown to pieces.

I leave my car and head upstairs a couple of floors. I find a nice secluded spot from which I have a good view of the entrance and I wait. Concealed from view by an advertising hording, I can see perfectly should the large van arrive and scrape under the low hanging height barrier.

All is still and peaceful as I wait and it is very much the calm before the storm. The peace before the terror. The silence before the bang. The emptiness before the intensity.

I sit and I wait, and I think of nothing and everything at the same time. I think mostly of Dex's big doe eyes and the need for me to return to them after all this, the need to not abandon him forever on that campsite.

Alice also fights for attention and I can't believe that she would be here today, not after everything, not after all the months of warnings and tip offs she's had from me. I can only assume she doesn't believe a word I've been saying about all of this, or that her brothers have dragged her here against her will?

As much as I'd like to think it was the latter, it's not.

All of me know she just doesn't think I'm right and that she was just playing along for the past few months. Perhaps she got caught up in the drama of the chase and the excitement, but couldn't bring herself to believe the calm, presentable man she saw, would be capable of what I was suggesting? It's hurtful, but I can hardly blame her. I, myself am still struggling to believe what I've seen, and I've had firsthand warnings from the man himself.

It just all seems too horrific to be true. It just all seems too much like so kind of movie plot, some kind of mad capped action movie. This kind of stuff doesn't play out in real life; these kinds of monsters just do not walk amongst us.

I think all this and then I see Phil's van pull into the parking lot and am reminded they very much do. This *is* real and this *is* happening.


The sight of the van, of the calm and composed man behind its wheel, and the knowledge of its cargo, sends my heart skipping. The tension and nerves begin to surface and the anxiety suddenly takes hold. I try to catch my breath as I see the van scrape through the low entrance and descend onto a lower floor.

In my hiding spot I hadn't realised the top level of the car park had slowly filled up with the early bird punters, there was no space for the van - not directly under the mall floor as I had foreseen.

This realisation rocks me as I head for the stairs that descend to the lower floors, chasing the vans as it descends. I had seen the van park on the top floor, the spot that would cause the maximum amount of damage to the shopping centre and cause the optimum number of casualties. I had seen all that happen - I had seen the chasm open up on the ground floor of the mall as the van exploded underneath it. And yet here it was in front of me - proof that I was wrong. He was forced to park lower down.

Perhaps through tardiness on his part or just through sheer luck, the spaces were all gone on the top floor and he was forced down onto the second basement level. Sure, the size of the bomb will still wreak havoc and tear up into the mall, many people will still perish - but things weren't playing out as I had seen.

My mind is racing with a million possibilities and theories as I reach the second level and see Phil Park up and leave his van. He has the same jacket on I've seen in my visions, and he has one hand in the left pocket as if protecting some precious cargo. I'd seen that right at least.

He walks away from me to an entrance to the shopping precinct at the other side of the car park, I sneak up to the van slowly as he leaves. He is striding away purposefully and with an intensity that is scaring me as I watch him go.

Pressing my ear to the van I hear nothing, tying to look inside I see nothing. It's just a van. A security guard wanders past and I say nothing.

IS there a bomb in this van? I'm can't be sure?

Am I right about all this? I'm can't be sure anymore. I have seen the same casual/sloppy outfit with concealed gun, I have seen this van and I have foreseen Phil's early arrival - but he wasn't parked here - he was parked upstairs.

Perhaps it's a minor detail, but it's enough to raise doubts in my already fragile mind, It's enough to send me sneaking after him across the car park and into the mall instead of raising the alarm.

I'm starting to think Alice was right all along, I'm starting to hope I won't die today.

# Chapter 40

It's now mid-morning. I've been trailing Phil around the mall for the past couple of hours. Nothing has happened again!

I've seen him have breakfast in the food court. I've seen him listen to the carol singers and donate £5. I've seen him sit by the giant Christmas tree in the centre of the mall and do nothing. He hasn't bought anything or even been in any shops. He's suspicious to me, but invisible to everybody else as the mall buzzes with festive life. All the while his hand has been glued inside his left jacket pocket where his pistol sits. He is anxious and nervous, but a nothingness to the general public.

All around us - as I watch him talking to some charity collector - is the spirit of Christmas. From the ceiling of the two storey mall dangle huge oversized bulbuls of glistening festive colours. A carpet of fairy lights covers the mall roof also and festive music fills the air. All around I see novelty Christmas jumpers, crackers, hats, chocolates, treats, and funny family gifts. A giant tree is the centre piece to the mall and it stretches up the two floors to the ceiling, some 20." A Santa's grotto sits nearby with a huge queue of inpatient children and fake, giant presents dotted around its queuing area.

I see women with masses of shopping bags and panicked men scrambling for forgotten gifts. I see overexcited children hopped up on candy, chocolates and biscuits, destined never too sleep tonight. I see them demanding excessive numbers of gifts in return for somewhat behaving - I see desperate parents granting such wishes at great financial expense to themselves, too stressed to care anymore.

The concerned faces of the debt ridden parents are all around me and the true spirit of Christmas is present. The consumer driven, spoiling, spending to excess, spirit of Christmas is here. The selfish give to receive - give because I have too - give because I should - attitude fills the air. Carollers sing and no-one listens because it doesn't mean anything to anyone anymore, not unless you can bottle it and give it as a gift to a relative you haven't seen since last Christmas.

I see all of this and then I see Alice and her brothers off in the distance and I start to panic again.

I see her split from her brothers as they head upstairs

and she heads off on the ground floor to a jewellery store. I look at Phil, talking and donating to the children's home, and I see Alice alone, entering a jewellery shop.

Flashes of the potential destruction and suffering wrestling with the normality of what is in front of me - then I turn my back on Phil and head for Alice. Just as I knew I would, just as I saw I would. I figure I have to get her to safety either way, if this is going to happen then I must save her, and if it doesn't then at least I would have put her out of harm's way regardless. I walk away from Phil and as I glance back a second later, he is already gone.

For now I must forget about him and get her out of here as quickly as I can. I sense it won't be easy. I sneak up behind her in the jewellery store.

All around are overpriced declarations of love, sparkling trinkets and adornments for lazy husbands and partners. Gold, silver, diamonds and precious stones - all at extortionate prices and all there to help men buy themselves a quiet life.

Alice is looking at lockets in a glass counter as I sidle up too her nervously. I've no idea how I'm going to make this happen, but I have to get this stubborn young girl out of this shopping centre instantly, all without alerting her brothers or causing public suspicion.

"I know what you're going to say Billy." She pronounces quietly without even looking up from the counter.

"…You're going to say that that man is here and were all going to die right?" She continues, scepticism laced in her voice, eyes fixed on some Platinum earrings that I was supposed to get her for Christmas.

I say yes, that's exactly what I going to say and I tell her that she has to leave here right now, and that I've seen him in the mall and I've seen his van parked underneath us. I say he has a gun and that he looks dangerous.

"Really, Billy? Because I saw him giving to a charity about 10 minute's ago." She looks at me like a patronising parent as she says this,

"…Oh and I asked for some earrings from Christmas remember? These will be fine?" She continues, pointing at a pair or silver hoops with and extortionate price tag, the same ones she waved in my face a few weeks ago.

Right now she is looking at me like she's sick of the sight of me.

Staring into her jaded eyes I struggle for a response. I

can see it on her face that she doesn't want to be listening to me right now, and that all of my stories are boring to her now.

It hurts but I attempt to reason with her. I tell her that even if I am wrong and all of this is in my mind - isn't it just worth leaving just in case? Go somewhere else, anywhere else and shop, why risk it? Why not just avoid this place entirely on the off chance I might have been right? That she can have the damn earrings right now if she agrees to leave immediately.

"Well, truth is Billy, I was keen to avoid this place, but then my brothers wanted to stop in quickly, so I couldn't refuse really - We'll be gone in an hour or so and never come back. And don't worry about a Christmas present eh….what's the point?" she says all this with a blasé and relaxed attitude that suggests she doesn't care anymore, perhaps a part of her wants to be here to see the carnage and the death, or on the other hand to rub it in my face when my claims fall flat?

With that she turns her back on me and moves further into the store, towards some silver broaches in a cabinet at the rear. I follow anxiously, nerves now really biting as Phil's whereabouts and actions are out of my sight and control. Grabbing at her shoulder, I snap at and say that she has to leave, raising my voice slightly to tell her I'm just trying to keep her safe and pleading with her to listen. The level of my voice raises a few glances in the store and I tell her that I have to get her to safety if my life depends on it.

"Yeah Billy ok, we will leave in a minute, give it a rest eh, its Christmas," she responds, looking at me like I'm and insane person that just needs pandering too until I shut up.

I stand there for a split second and I am angry and confused. Why is she ignoring me, why is she palming me off, why is the women I love paying me no attention? I'm furious that I'm trying to save this women's life, yet she can barely bring herself to look in my eyes anymore.

Am I really that far gone?

Am I really so insane and consumed by this that Alice, my one confident and supporter, has nothing but patronising words and resentment for me?

Am I really so insane that I grab her by the arm and drag her from the store, screaming and protesting, as I force her from the shop?

Am I really so consumed that I turn the collective

attention of an entire place towards me as I grab at this young beauty by the arm and appear to throw her from the jewellery store?

Am I really so delusional and panic stricken that the mall security is called against me as I try to drag Alice towards the mall exit as she kicks and screams?

Yes, yes, I am - I really am that far gone now.

Right now the security at the mall is being told I'm the danger as I seemingly attack this innocent young lady.

Right now Phil is wandering towards his wife as she enters the lingerie shop off in the distance. Right now everyone in the world thinks I am the terrorist.

## Chapter 41

So all around me drama happens.

Every shopper, passerby and staff member in the immediate vicinity have all stopped to look at me. To be fair I am dragging a young lady, some 10 years my junior, forcefully from a shop by her arm as she protests and struggles against me.

Perhaps I do look like a would-be kidnapper and/or attacker, perhaps I do look like I'm about to drag this pretty young thing away and rape her? Maybe to everyone casually glancing as the scene erupts, I do look like a dangerous assailant on the verge of a horrific Yule tide attack? Everyone is probably right to assume that I'm the danger and threat amongst them despite a 2 tonne fertiliser bomb sits beneath our feet's.

If I had time, any time at all, and I thought I could reason my way out of this, then I would try. But time is of the essence as Phil moves un-opposed somewhere amongst the crowds. Desperate time's call for desperate measures and right now I'm as desperate as they come. Sure I look a danger right now but this is for the greater good, this is for

Alice, this is for her family and her brothers. This is for the assembled crowd that are circling and baying at me as I attempt to drag Alice across the mall floor towards the exit doors.

This is for all of them - they just don't know it yet.

I can hear the following things being screamed as the voices escalate and erupt around me, all the time trying desperately to ignore them as I attempt to force Alice to safety;

"LET HER GO,"

"SECURITY! SECURITY! HE'S TRYING TO RAPE THAT GIRL!"

"YOU LET HER GO OR I'LL RIP YOUR DICK OFF,"

"AHHHH PEADO, PEADO!"

"SOMEONE CALL THE COPS!"

"BILLY, WHAT ARE YOU DOING, YOU'VE GONE CRAZY,"

"QUICK STOP THAT MAN!"

"HE'S GOING TO KILL THAT WOMEN!"

"PLEASE STOP BILLY, YOUR GOING TO GET YOURSELF LOCKED UP, THIS HAS GONE TOO FAR NOW."

"LISTEN MATE, WHATEVER SHE HAS DONE, SHE DOESN'T DESERVE THIS, LET HER BE",

"IT'S CHRISTMAS EVE! LET HER GO,"

"BILLY MY BROTHERS ARE COMING. PLEASE JUST LET ME GO AND RUN. I'LL EXPLAIN EVERYTHING, JUST GO."

Through the din, the chaos, the struggle, I hear Alice say some of these things, but am too consumed with mortal panic to comprehend or take them in.

My focus is on the exit doors, on forcing my way through the ever increasing throng, on saving her despite the rejection, doubts and current hatred towards me. This cannot all have been for nothing and even if I can't stop Phil and this place is about to blow - I must save someone. I must save Alice from what she doesn't think is coming. Fuck everyone else, all of those who are turning on me as I edge ever closer to the mall exit doors.

I take a few punches to the back of the head and a passerby or two are now attached to my outstretched arm along with Alice. I am relying on feats of strength I didn't realise I was capable off, as I drag Alice and a couple of strangers towards the light with me, inch by inch.

I avert my laser like gaze off of the exit doors momentarily and glance behind me, I see the following madness: Alice, screaming and clawing at my arm as my vice like grip clasps her upper arm, a throng of shoppers all screaming various things and trying to grab at my arm and break my hold, shopping bags are scattered across the mall floor in my wake, a child is crying as his mother drags him along with her as she chases after me shouting. I see several disinterested passersby, I see a young man walk directly past us in the opposite direction - oblivious to the scene as he texts and walks, another oblivious young adult has earphones in and cannot comprehend anything outside his immediate perimeter.

Through the war and the madness I also see Chad steaming after us across the mall floor, closely followed by Bret. They are both very angry. The sight of these behemoths closing in on me momentarily panics me, but I'm resolved to make it out of here before the beatings and the explosions. I focus back on the exits doors, now some 20 feet away, and pull harder against the mob behind me.

Seconds later I hear some deep guttural roars that I assume are Chad and some heavy footsteps as he closes in.

"MY SISTER," someone screams as a diving body hits me hard in the back and sends me, and the attached mass, tumbling to the hard floor. I assume I am knocked out by this and receive several punches to the face because the next thing I see is

Chad straddled above me, directing his enormous fist towards my face. I see all this through one eye because my left eye has closed over and swollen since I was last conscious.

I shield myself from the impending blow and then do something I never thought I was capable of - I swung back. I threw an enraged, venting right fist, back up at Chad's mutinous face and caught him squarely on the jaw. Either he was so surprised by this, or he has a desperately fragile jaw, but it sends him tumbling backwards off of me and I am free to get to my feet. Albeit shakily, but I stand none the less. In front of me on the floor Chad lays back on his haunches and stares at me with shocked admiration, rubbing his tender jaw with what I think is a grudging respect in his eyes.

Other things I see right now are a circle of spectators surrounding us, some gathering their forgotten belongings from the floor. Bret consoling a distraught Alice as she sobs into his chest, a couple of security guards running hastily towards us; a broken pile of baubles littering the floor in a shingle of ornate glass; A few old women tutting and shaking their wrinkly fingers in my direction; various other women with prams and young kids screaming hatred at me.

I see all this and I realise I might have fucked this up again.

God knows where Phil is and if and when the rest of his plan will be put into place, but I'm not sure how this is helping my cause right now? What the security guards will have in store for me I've no idea - but any type or reprimand or questioning will seriously compromise my position.

I glance to the exit. Outside the crisp, cold winter brightness encourages me, tantalises me, beckons me too it.

I can run from this. I can flee the scene and get away from everyone right now? Perhaps sneak back in an hour or two when things have settled, try and do my thing then, sneak into the car park covertly and intervene if I still can?

I could do that, but by then it could be too late. I can't run now, I could be endangering everyone if I did that. I mean they all hate me and think I'm the threat they need protecting from, but if I run now and then the bomb goes off - I've failed miserably and all these people who hate me will be a pile of corpses.

I'm a fool, an idiot, a reckless maniac, a blunt headed buffoon - but redemption is still there to be had if I can stay within the vicinity.

The security guards push through the line of spectators before me and I realise it's time to face the music, time to lighten the load and tell someone something, try to make them listen this time.

Desperate time's call for desperate measures; It's time to try and explain all this and hope it's not all too late.

# Chapter 42

So two security guards stand in front of me; Decked in typically grey and dour uniforms with big bold SECURITY badges on their chests and hands on hips to establish authority. They have thick black belts around their waists that hold nothing more than a pair of cuffs and a radio, but this still makes them feel infinitely superior. There are no weapons to be seen so I'm feeling a little less threatened than I perhaps should be.

Over their shoulders stand Brad, Chad, and a still distraught Alice. She is being consoled by her brothers as they shout and scream things in my direction. The assembled crowd has been ushered away and the din has somewhat calmed, but I am currently being fixed with a look that suggests I'm not far away from a jail cell once again.

"You wanna explain yourself my friend?" One of these guards finally proposes, with a voice that suggests he's already made his mind up about the situation.

"HE TRIED TO FUCKING RAPE HER!" Screams Chad as he rushes forward towards me once again, nostrils flared and fists clenched. Such is the size and momentum of this hulking beast, he breaks the line of protection created by the two guards and strikes a wild forearm against my right leg as I swerve away from him. His wild, trunk like arm, sailing through the barricade and deadening my upper thigh. I stumble backwards and hop around in pain whilst one of the guards drags Chad away and puts some distance between us on the mall floor, taking with him Bret and Alice for their side of the story.

"So you are going to explain why he's trying to kill you?" The remaining guard continues after I've regained some composure, producing a small pad and pencil from his pocket whilst he waits.

I try to settle on my throbbing leg and take stock of just what I'm about to say to this man. This confused, irritated guy is just trying to do a hard day's work and keep the peace before he can go home for Christmas - now he has this to deal with. This naïve, stern man, thinks this situation can be broken down onto a tiny notepad with a miniature pencil! This honest man thinks he is keeping these people safe in this bustling mall, this guard cannot dream of the real terror that will unfold here today.

I compose myself, settle my bruised leg back on the floor,

and simply tell him that this mall will be blown up by a terrorist in a matter of hours, maybe minutes, perhaps second, and I was trying to save her because I love her, I say.

The man doesn't write any of this on his pocket sized pad; instead he simply freezes and looks up at me like I'm delivering some life shattering news.

Jaw is agape. Eyes are wide and wild.

From the look on his face right now I can tell he's struggling to comprehend just what has come out of my mouth. On his face I can see a mixture of confusion, shock, disbelief, doubt and terror. Whilst his eyes fix mine and his gaze deepens, I can tell he's looking for answers, looking into my soul to try and comprehend how to deal with this news, how to deal with me? Am I a madman? Am I the terrorist? Was that a threat, a promise or just wild fantasy? Is this rough, tramp like man with questionable hygiene, really worth listening too?

I can see all these things running through his mind and I sympathise with him because he's normally only dealing with people nicking CD's. I sympathise, because all he wanted was a quiet day at work before the Christmas holidays can begin.

He's probably desperate to go home to his wife, maybe a kid or two, and curl up under the tree and trinkets before the celebrations begin in the morning.

"I'm sorry…" he finally continues, catching his breath as the words leak out.

I repeat.

I tell him there is a man who is planning to blow up this mall today, and that a transit van is parked on the second lower floor of the multi-storey and it has a two tonne fertiliser bomb in it. I tell him this man's name is Phillip Green and he is in here right now with a gun and is probably taking his wife hostage as we speak. I tell him I was trying to save Alice because I love her and didn't want her to die in the explosion - I was going to raise the alarm once I'd gotten her to safety I say, we have to do something I say - right now I say.

The man writes the word 'BOMB??' in capitals on his paper and I wonder what good he possibly thinks that's going to do to help?

Still fixing my gaze and even more confused than he was thirty seconds before, the man suddenly calls out.

"DAVE!" He yelps in a tone of voice that is both nervous

and sceptical at the same time. Evidently, Dave is the other guard speaking to Alice and her brother; he turns away from them and heads towards us upon hearing his name. From the look on his face he is equally bemused by the situation and the side of the story he's been told.

My man raises his child like pad with the word 'BOMB??' on it to his friend Dave as he joins him by his side. He is still staring at me bemused all the while as he does this.

"Bomb…?" Dave pronounces and looks at me with the same bemusement his college hasn't been able to shake off since this conversation began. Now I have to explain everything once more to Dave as his friend appears to be speechless at the revelations and cannot relay the details himself.

Over their shoulders I can see Alice and her brothers starting to calm and compose themselves. The smug look on Bret's face tells me they have been weaving some pretty inflammatory stories about me, and this could be a hard sell. No doubt I've been painted as some kind of paedophile and rampaging alcoholic, whose been in jail before and has been keeping Alice hostage for the post months. Not all of that is true, but some of it is.

So I tell Dave everything I told his mate - and the pair

of them look at me, then each other, then Dave glances back towards Alice and her brothers, then back to me.

"They said you're a drunk and you were going to rape her?" Dave quizzes as he points across to the others. At this point I break it down for Dave - again! I get irate and impatient as I cannot just stand here when chaos lays beneath us, I can feel the end coming and it scares me, so I raise my voice considerably.

Sharply and forcefully I tell him that I may well be all of the things they said I am, but I'm also right. I tell him that I will show them the van, I will take them directly too it and point out Phil on the CCTV so they can intercept. I tell him them that they are free to lock me up and charge me with assault, battery, or just disorderly behaviour, afterwards - but first just listen to me, I plead.

I tell Dave this floor will be littered with the blood of the many children currently waiting to see Santa, and that even if you don't believe me, just humour me for 10 minutes. Just follow me, cuffed if you have too, and I will show you why I was so desperate to get my former lover to safety.

I tell him, with a cold dead look in my eyes and a calm, composed tone - that I can see the future and I have seen the devil blow a hole in the very floor were stood upon.

Now Dave looks at me with his jaw on the floor.

Right now I'm pretty sure I'm going to die right here with these two staring at me.

I can't be sure but I think at least two or three minutes pass in silence as these two guys try to fathom a course of action.

"Rigghhhtt, OK, OK, I tell you what, put these on for us….", Dave finally breaks in, reaching for his cuffs as he speaks, "…And we will go and find this bomb you speak off and see just how crazy you may or may not be." He clamps a cuff across my left wrist as he speaks, scared and irritated at the same time.

A small crowd has now re-assembled around us all and over his shoulder I can see Alice looking at me with a sad but resigned look on her face. Right now she's looking at me like I'm a mistake, like I am insane and this is the natural conclusion to our whirlwind adventure. Right now I'm looking back at her like I hate her for not listening to me.

Dave clamps the second cuff across my right wrist and starts to lead me away with a soft right hand on my back, my hands safely cuffed together in front of my groin.

"Come on then my friend, you lead the way, but were stocking mace so don't make any drastic moves." As he talks his speechless friend joins me to my right side and we start making or way across the mall.

Around me I can see disappointed, disgusted and horrified faces. These are the people I'm trying to save, these scowling punters looking at me like I'm the one who's trying to steal Christmas. Around me the din of Christmas carols ring ever louder and I think the soundtrack to my death may be some tinny, over produced, novelty festive tune.

As I walk I start to think the floor could give way any second and the explosion will tear me limb from limb. As I walk I take one last look at Alice and think I will never see her again, I start to think that I love her and I want to die for her, with her, because things will never return to what there were between us. Things are now forever changed, and she is lost too me either way - so why not die with her in close proximity like this?

I start to think a lot of things as I am frog marched across the mall towards the car park. How right now I'm pretty famous in this mall, I'm making the news, and right now people are Tweeting about me!

Right now I am Schrödinger's cat - I am both alive and dead at the same time. Me and everyone else, staring down, across and around at me - are all about to die and all about to live.

I think all this nonsense then I see Phil escorting his wife from the lingerie store up on the second floor above us. She is scared; he is calm and is prodding her in the back with his gun - apparently oblivious to the scene I have caused, or perhaps using it as cover?

I catch my breath. I am relieved that there is still a chance.

I stop walking.

I point with my conjoined wrists up at the second floor, at Phil and his terrified wife, as he tries to rush her away, gun barely concealed at her back.

"HE HAS A BOMB! ITS HIM, HE HAS A BOMB IN HIS VAN. RUN. HE'S GOING TO KILL US ALL!" I scream.

All around me chaos and confusion erupts.

# Chapter 43

Upon hearing this everything stopped. Everyone - hundreds of shoppers - turn to gape at me. Carollers fall silent, mothers freeze and gasp, teenagers actually look up from their phones, the world around me stops for a split second.

Phil also heard this and has also stopped dead in his tracks. Barely containing his wife as she struggles for freedom against his vice like grip, he stares down over the second floor banisters at me, cuffed and being escorted on the ground floor of the mall below.

Our eyes meet for what feels like an eternity.

He's staring down at me, I'm staring back up at him; Stillness and silence all around; Hundreds of concerned eyes on me and him. In his eyes I can see a mixture of hurt, betrayal, guilt, confusion, anger, hostility and resentment. In my eyes he would see desperation, resolve, fear and terror.

What strikes me most about the cold dead eyes of this pending terrorist is the scale of disappointment betrayed in them. With eyebrows slightly widened, his face tells me he thought I'd let him get away with all this. I can see he was completely convinced that he had scared me off, and that I was too much of a coward to intervene - a beating in a public house toilet and a subsequent arrest was all it would take. I can see in his face that he was completely convinced he would never see me again after last time. Such is his puppy dog; hurt expression that I almost feel like I have let him down.

I think all this and then I see the barrel of his stubby pistol pointed towards me.

My heart stops.

Everything stops again.

Then his gun explodes and my ears feel like they start to bleed.

Pandemonium is now is full flow in the mall. All around me shoppers are running for their lives, people are fleeing with or without their purchases. The queue at the Grotto instantly dissipates as terrified parents drag their children away. These children are confused and upset as they will no longer get to see old St Nick today.

I feel a warm spray across my left cheek and it's not until I glance to my left that I realise Dave's head has exploded. On the floor next to me I can see his well built and stocky body, adorned with standard issue security guard kit that is well pressed and presented. Dave was a smart man who took his job seriously and worked long and hard for the cause. From the neck up a blank, lifeless face looks back at me - a small red dot in the centre of the forehead seeps a small amount of blood. His dead black eyes pierce my soul as I realise the lethal nature of a bullet first hand and feel the warm red liquid consequences of one, on my face. Underneath Dave's head, a small pool of blood begins to form and seep out from the back of his head. This red puddle flows into the cracks and grooves of the flooring and spreads outwards across the tiles in an almost perfect circle around Dave's lifeless head.

Right now I'm looking down at this dead body and thinking many things. About how this guy was alive and well literally seconds go, about how I was at the mercy of this cadaver a minute or two ago, about how quickly life can be extinguish and about how you would even begin to explain this to his family?

I think all this as another gunshot pierces my eardrums.

I glance up at Phil, stunned and shocked to still be alive. Then I glance to my right and I see another body, the dying figure of guard No.2. This time blood is seeping profusely from this man's chest as he gasps hopelessly for breath. His eyes are wide and panic stricken and he knows this is not a battle that he will not win. I can almost see the life flashing before his very eyes as he takes even more strained breaths.

Right here, right now, this man is dying at my feet.

I spend a split second considering what I can do? What the alcoholic, handcuffed psychic, can do for this dying man whose been shot in the chest? Whose clasped hands over his torso are doing nothing to prevent the thick crimson fluid seeping out and taking his life with it? I spend another split second thinking if any of the first aid I learned in scouts may be of use right now?

Right now I feel useless and a bit neglectful. I kneel at this man's side, Dave's partner in crime, and place both of my cuffed hands on his bloody hands.

They are cold and warm at the same time.

I can feel his heart stopping.

I can feel his blood oozing.

I can feel the end of the world coming. His hands remain lifeless and stone like, desperately pressed across the wound as if it will help. I look into his eyes and realise that life has already left his body. Riga-mortis was setting in almost instantly.

I look into his soulless eyes and ponder what to say. See in the movies everyone's composed and controlled when someone dies in front of them. Theirs always quip, a word of solace or condolence for the fallen pier, the hero will always say something noble to thank the dead for the ultimate sacrifice.

But this isn't a film, so I don't say anything. I just look at the corpse and feel the blood coagulate and become sticky at my cuffed hands.

Right now I feel useless and pathetic. Right now Phil is winning, nay - Phil has already won. Right now I feel like a failure.

I get to my feet and stare back up at Phil.

I am unaware of time and how long this has all taken, but I look back up to find him still standing there with his gun raised and pointed in my direction.

It's safe to assume that he wasn't trying to kill me with the previous two shots, and they reached their intended targets - no-one can be that poor a shot. Both reached their intended destinations with devastating effect and now it's my turn.

Right now I'm about to die. Right now, as he stares down at me, gun raised, finger on the trigger - I want him to kill me. I am now forever changed by the events of the past few seconds and for the rest of my life, the cold dead eyes of the security guards will be in my nightmares. I am not the same man I was a few seconds ago and I'm not sure I want to live with this kind of weight on my soul. After all they were only in the line of fire because of me. If I hadn't of shown up, they may have died in the resulting explosion, or they may not have, but they certainly wouldn't have been escorting me as I interrupted a gun wielding maniac.

All around me chaos and silence is breaking out in equal measure. I can see crowds fleeing, I can see tears, I can see people on the edge of life - but I can hear nothing; Nothing except a slight ringing in both ears. Temporarily deafened by the dual gunshots, the Christmas music no longer invades my consciousness.

I glance over to where Alice and her brothers once were just in time to see her being dragged from the scene by them. She is kicking and screaming and seemingly intent on trying to come to my rescue. I see panic, fear and terror in her eyes, the type you would expect from someone about to lose a loved one. I see her desperate to save me and desperate to keep me alive. I see her flailing wildly against her restrainers, intent on risking her life too save me. I see tears and terror contort her face and I think I see her mouth 'I love you' but I can't be sure.

This realisation – that she does care when it really comes down to it – fills me with a strange serenity as I feel Phil's attention turn to me with his deadly pistol.

A gun is trained on my head.

A finger is on the trigger.

I am about to die and am somehow happy with this.

Happy to know that Alice cared after all and that she will be safe.

Mission accomplished.


All this is true, but just then Phil's barely contained wife suddenly breaks free from his grasp and dashes for her life, sending him stumbling off balance in the process. A bullet explodes into a glass shop behind me as his aim is sent haywire.

Phil scarpers after his wife on the open floor above me. I watch him run. His attention no longer trained on me. I watch her run faster than him and hope that she may reach safety.

I watch all of this from the floor below and I know I've been given a second chance. That I was millimetres - split seconds - away from a bullet being lodged in my forehead. I was saved by a blonde housewife whose own attempts to save herself, inadvertently save me. I have another chance to stop this. I have another bite of the cherry. I watch as Phil, running at full pace across the second floor, raises his gun and shoots his wife in the back of her leg. She is thrown to the floor and out of my view.

I've got a second chance I think, and I can still do something I think.

## Chapter 44

Its moments later now and I'm knelt at the side of Dave's corpse. My ears are still ringing and my body is trembling. The adrenaline and shock of the last few minutes taking their toll, and I am visibly quivering as if I'm naked at the North Pole. This is making the process of retrieving the handcuff keys and unlocking them even trickier than it would have been anyway, I'm not Houdini after all.

Just now I saw Phil throw his injured wife through the doors into the car park lift area, he had retrieved her from the floor after he shot her and was heading down in the lift that leads down into the car park. Evidently he is still intent on carrying out his plan.

This is despite the fact he has already murdered two people and his wife may well die from the gunshot wound if she doesn't get medical attention soon. This is despite the fact I have raised an alarm of sorts, and thus, the numbers inside the mall are now significantly lower than they would have been beforehand. This realisation fills me with a sense of pride and achievement as I finally fumble a small key into the cuffs and break out of their binds - I have saved people.

It seems my haphazard, uncoordinated and reckless

behaviour has actually saved the lives of many people. As I get to my feet and quickly survey the scene I can see stillness and peace.

I can still hear nothing but a dull ringing in both ears, but from what I see, peace has fallen upon the mall and the crowds have disappeared. Some are still fighting at the nearby exits as the sheer volume of people attempt to squeeze through the bottle necks, but generally the place looks empty.

No more carol singers, no more queues at the concessions stands and Grotto, no more busy punters swarming around like bees, no more Alice, no more brothers.

I see emptiness, peace, serenity. I see success and achievement. I see the scatter possessions of the fled, dotted and sprayed across the floor. Granted there are two corpses at my feet, but still - I see relative peace and success.

I have saved a lot of people, but most importantly I have saved Alice. I saw her being forcefully removed from the scene by her brothers, they are keeping her safe, they are doing their job well and maybe she is safe because of me also? Maybe my wild and desperate actions resulted in her leaving a bomb site, one she may still have been in if I hadn't have intervened? I think I have saved her and that maybe, just maybe, my life wasn't a complete waste after all?

I've made a change today in the lives of numerous people, they may never really know what I did for them - I may just be passed off as a madman at the mall who attacked a young girl - but I know in my heart of hearts that I made a huge difference today.

With renewed vigour and confidence, I start on towards the stairwell doors with free hands, the doors I was escorting my fallen captors too moments earlier.

But I take a couple of steps and then I stop. Do I need to carry on? Do I need to do anymore? Haven't I done enough in the past few minutes? I risked my life and cleared out a bomb site. I had a bullet graze my ear for these people; I stared down the barrel of a gun and was given a reprieve, so surely I've done enough? If the explosion still happens there will be no one here to suffer from it surely?

I turn around and scour the mall for signs of life, for reasons for me to take further risks, for lives that still need saving. Phil's wife is not enough - sure I don't want her to die - but I can't risk my life again for this one random woman I've never met.

Right now I want to run outside and find Alice.

Right now I want to see no reason to pursue this game of cat and mouse.

Right now I'm scared I may not be so lucky the next time there's a gun pointed in my direction.

Right now I want to leave.

Then I look through the stillness, the emptiness and the peace I thought I was surrounded by, and I find a hundred more reasons to carry on. I look harder and see the mall worker cradled down in her snack stand, I look deep into the various stores and see all the employees sheltering in various hiding places, I see shoppers fleeing into the toilet blocks, I see Santa and his elves huddled safely in their Grotto.

The mall may be a lot less crowded than it was before gunshots were fired, but it seems a lot of people simply hid instead of fleeing. A lot of people are still in harm's way. A lot of people don't know the real threat is a 2 tonne bomb beneath the floor and that crouching down in a popcorn stand isn't going to save you. A lot of people though a gun was the danger when I fact it's a huge bomb.

This place will still crumble in moments and all these stealthy types will still die. Right now I'm angry at them and part of me wants to let them all die for being so stupid.

Right now I want to leave, but I have to stay.

So I turn and run through the exit doors and ascend into the depths of hell that waits below, I still have a job to do.

## Chapter 45

I'm astonished when I reach the second lower level and seek out the van. I expect these lower parking levels to be empty after the horror of what has happened above, I expect to see rows of empty cars sat in silence as a terrorist scuttles amongst them with a bleeding woman at his side.

What I don't expect to see are cars speeding to get out, careering wildly up the levels and through the rows of parked cars. I don't expect to see families, grief stricken and panicked, behind the wheels of their family motors as they try and flee the danger. I didn't think anyone would even contemplate returning to their cars after the murders had taken place above, but evidently a lot have. Evidently more people than you would expect/hope, seem to hold their cars so dear to them that they must first return to rescue them, before exiting the scene of a double murder.

Sure there is a madman on the loose, sure he has murdered two people in full view of the assembled masses, yes he's clearly out to kill anyone who gets in his way - but let's not leave the Lexus behind eh.

I despair at the behaviour of these people, but in their minds I guess a car will get them away from danger a lot quicker than running will? If your outrunning a maniac, a car probably is better I guess - just as long as he doesn't shoot you before you get to it. I scowl and dodge one such car, as it swerves up a nearby ramp and continues past me to the upper floors and the exit, a terrified mother behind the wheel.

Off in the distance, across a sea of empty cars, I can see Phil's van. Its back doors are wide open and it is rocking slightly from side to side in its bay, rocking in a way that suggests violent behaviour must be taking place inside. I assume he is beating or raping her in there, such is the undulation of the vehicle.

Ears now ringing less and some hearing returning, but hands starting to tremble once again, I start to make my way past the amassed parked vehicles, keeping ducked against the wall and out of sight as I do so. As I move every part of me is ignoring the fact it could explode at any second, killing me instantly.

I can't see inside from here, and I move so stealthily that he wouldn't see me if he suddenly appeared out of the open doors either. I'm hopefully staying out of sight and out of mind. As I creep ever closer to the rocking van, sneaking past overpriced expensive cars as I move, it suddenly dawns on me that I have no plan other than get close enough to somehow stop the explosion.

I mean, I have to be on the scene to do something, but what that something is I'm not really sure? I can't diffuse bombs unfortunately, so that option is a non starter. I also can't take down an armed maniac with my bare hands, so that's out of the window too.

I guess, as I sneak past the bonnet of an oversized 4x4 truck, I have to get hold of the detonator and run? It's not much of a plan I know, but it's all I can muster at the minute as I scramble past the boot of people carrier, nearing the undulating van, its suspension rocking heavily. How and when I get hold of this detonator I'm not sure, but if I can get hold of the switch then the bomb can't be triggered. I'm assuming. I'm also hoping that I can do all this before he blows everything into smithereens and also, before he murders me.

Alternately I muse, as a red sports car is rounded, I could try and buy some time before the police arrive on the scene. A rapid armed response team must be on their way, and if I can stall this somehow, then I can pass the mantle onto the professionals.

It is feasible option, but then we have a hostage situation on our hands with a terrorist who's still likely to detonate once they get here. He's nothing to lose, so at that point their arrival probably won't bother him all that much, he would just have a few more victims.

No, I have to get that detonator - by whatever means - I conclude as a blue hatchback stands between me and the shaking van. I round it and sidle up to the vans rear wheels, its rear doors still wide open offering me plenty of cover from the incumbents.

Strangely, now I'm closer and within muffled hearing distance of the action inside the van, I feel safer. My heart, which has been beating furiously, now for some time, has started to settle as I kneel at the rear wheel of the van and listen as best as I can. I feel safer and calmer because I can just about hear what's going on inside and from this I know the bomb isn't due to go off just yet.

I have a couple more minutes left to live at least - I know this because Phil is raping his wife in there right now.

With my hearing slowly returning, but still compromised, these are some of the things I hear when waiting patiently at the vehicle rear. I hear Phil shouting various obscenities with an exhausted, out of breath tone, as he violently gets some revenge on his estranged wife. I hear a women's voice crying and protesting. I hear what I assume are barrels, bouncing off of each other and letting out humble ding's, I hear the axles of the vehicle protesting as it's thrown from side to side by the action inside.

I hear ticking that at first I think is the bomb, but then realise I had my watch closer to my face than I realised.

I listen in and think that this could well be the perfect moment to make a dash for the detonator. He's clearly occupied and won't have his eyes on it at this moment, so I might have a chance?

Very slowly, with a view to try and get some kind of visual inside the van, I lower myself onto the cold, hard concrete flooring. I carefully crawl up past the back wheel of the van and use the wide open back doors as cover. Seconds pass and the continued violence in the van tells me I'm still undetected, so I crane my neck out under the back doors I'm currently sheltered by.

I don't see a lot from this obscure worm's eyes vantage point, but what I do see terrifies me. I see the back of Phil's body, trousers round his ankles and bare ass exposed to the world. He is stood against the adjacent side of the van. He has his wife pinned up against a barrel of explosive lining the inside walls of the van. He has his gun pressed under her throat as he does this.

I can't see her whole face or expression, but right now I assume she would rather be dead. I can't see his face, but I'm guessing after the shame of this, he'd rather be dead too.

From my vantage point I can see about 5 of these barrels lined up against one side of the van and a couple more at the front of the van. I can only assume there are 5 more lined up against the other side of the van closest to me, but obscured from view.

There is enough here to blow a hole in the earth.

I scour the inside of the van for signs of the detonator, but nothing is visible from where I am. I slide out under a bit further for more insight. Still nothing!

I edge out a little more, my head and shoulders now clearly visible if Phil turns around. I still can't see anything or reach any detonator or potential weapon. If I had anything to hand, a bat or shovel for example, Phil could be easily knocked out right now with a single blow to the back of the head, but there's nothing around.

For a moment I contemplate using my fists then I realise I'm not a boxer and can't just knock out armed men with a single punch. Then I edge out too far and I hear a gasp from the van.

A gasp that tells me I've been seen.

Everything freezes for a second. For a second time stops and I wait for the bullet to hit the back of my skull as I lay face down on the floor at the back of the van.

It doesn't.

Instead I hear a woman's voice.

"Phil, Phil….kiss me please….please kiss Me." Phil's wife says as she grabs his jaw and sticks her lips to his. Up until now she has been as distraught and emotional as anyone would be whilst being violently raped at gunpoint by a former partner, all the while surrounded by explosives - but she says this in a lustful, seductive and surprised manner that startles both Phil and I.

I glance up as I hear their lips connect and I look straight into her eyes. With hands clasped around Phil's head and shoulders, and her lips locked to his, she looks down at me with wide, panicked eyes.

Eyes so wide and eyebrows so raised - that I know she's communicating with them. The kind of eyes that tell me I've been stupid and would have been killed if Phil was facing the other way. The kind of eyes that tell me to hide again and wait, be patient and try to save us all properly instead of crawling around on the floor. The kind of eyes that tell me she's glad I'm here and that she knows what we have to do, that she will stall this and do whatever she can to save herself and everyone else.

The kind of eyes that tell me we're now in alliance.

I crawl back out from under the door and return to my knelling point at the rear wheel, safe from view as the carnage continues in the back of the van, but now in tag team with Phil's distraught wife.

Decades seem to pass as I crouch there waiting, but my watch reveals it was in fact 2 minutes. 2 minutes it takes for Phil to finally come and start crying.

Then I listen intently as Phil's wife, my ally, gets to works. A conversation that's a mixture of a calm, composed, measured voice - with an erratic, manic and psychotic one.

"Come on Phil, why are you doing this? This isn't you?"

"I'm doing this because you left me, after all I've done for you, you discarded me to the scrap heap for no good reason. I'm not doing this - YOU'RE DOING THIS."

"Phil please don't do this, there is no need. I just need some space, maybe there will be a time when I'm ready to come home, but I just need a bit of space to live a little. Please don't kill me."

"YOU DON'T GET THE RIGHT ANYMORE TO TELL ME WHAT TO DO WOMAN - I SHOULD BLOW YOU HEAD OFF RIGHT NOW."

"PHIL PLEASE, PLEASE - please don't kill me, don't blow everything up, we can work this out, I just need some space."

"Why, WHY! Why do you need some space?"

"I just do Phil, A women needs to feel special and cherished for a while; I need to feel young and attractive again. Just let me do that for a while, let me get it out of my system, then I'll come home to you."

"Why can't you do that with me? Why have you got to fuck HIM?"

"Phil, don't, come on - this isn't you, you just killed two men back there and shot me! Why are you doing this? I'm bleeding - LOOK!"

"BECAUSE I AM KATY! THAT'S WHY! I'm doing this because nothing matters anymore and I want to make the world burn. I want everyone to suffer with me. I'm doing this because I can and no-one can stop me!"

"But Phil, why? You're a calm and gentle man, why do this to everyone?"

"KATY STOP! Stop trying to convince me not to do this. Stop trying to talk me out of it. It's gone too far now - I've killed two men. I'm not going back to life now. It's over. IT'S ALL OVER!"

"NO PHIL WAIT. I HAVE SOMETHING TO TELL YOU."

"Tell me? TELL ME! IT'S TOO LATE FOR THAT WOMAN."

"NO PHIL, PHIL, I'M PREGNANT!"

I'm listening to all of this and waiting for the world around me to turn into fire. Phil is wild and erratic and her desperate attempts to deter him only seem to be making things worse. That was until she said she was pregnant and for some reason he believed her.

"Pregnant, pregnant really?"

"Yes Phil and it's yours. Please don't do this. We can fix this and be together again. Please just stop all this. Feel my stomach, there, feel……its yours Phil, you're going to be a father again if you just stop all this."

"No you're lying - you're lying, I can't feel anything.

You think I'm that stupid? You think I'm going to fall for that? You really think you can stop all this just with a simple little lie?"

"NO, NO, its true Phil, believe me. I had a scan last week and was going to tell you, but wasn't sure how you would react, but it's true. It will bring us back together - we can be a family again".

As an impartial third party I can tell two things from this exchange, despite not being able to actually see either of them.

One, that the desperation and panic in the ladies voice tells me this is all a huge lie. That she's clearly not pregnant and this is one last ditch attempt to assuage the madman with the bomb. And two, that despite a ting of hope in his voice, deep down he knows she's lying to him. He knows, but he's enjoying fantasising about it for a minute or so, enjoying the thought of their reconciled marriage and the joy of a new baby - but he's not really buying it and it's not long before he explodes again.

"YOU LIAR. THERE IS NO CHILD. THERE IS NO US. THERE IS NO HOPE SO DON'T FUCKING LIE TO ME."

"No Phil, Phil, No, please..."

His wife screams and the van lurches wildly as action breaks out inside. For a moment I think an explosion will tear the world to pieces any second, but when it doesn't, I come to realise he is beating her in there.

I can hear the sickening sound of fists flying and a woman cowering in terror. Every fibre of me wants to jump out and intervene, but I hold my counsel as I would be acting blind and putting everything in serious jeopardy.

This beating continues for a minute or so and the van lurches from side to side as a body is thrown, struck and beat around inside it. Outside, such is the wild shaking of the van; I'm battered and nudged to the floor. I hear Phil scream obscenities, his wife cower in pain and I hear the gallons of petrol slosh around in their barrels as the van rocks.

I start to get anxious and concerned that he will simply kill her and blow everything up, and that she won't get a chance to do anything, waiting for her isn't working. She may be knocked out, unconscious, or murdered before he has a clear run to complete his plans.

I lower myself back onto my belly and slide out under the van doors once again, desperate to see something, anything.

After all how much attention is he paying to a detonator or a gun whilst beating his wife? This may be my window.

I crane my neck under in time to see a flowing lock of blonde hair cascade down out of the back of the van, dangling down from the vans floor in front of me.

From my worms eye view I see the back of Phil's wife's head, her hair dangling down inches from my face, hanging off of the back of the van. I see Phil's enraged hands clasped around her neck as his wife is pinned helplessly to the floor, her head hanging out of the back of the van, her neck arching badly. I see him straddling her prostrate body as he violently chokes her. I see her frantic hands flailing around, trying desperately to grab at the demon above her. I see a women dying mere inches from my face and I don't know what to do.

I see Phil's devilish, contorted face. A man possessed with pure rage and hatred as he sets about extinguishing his soul mates life. A man's whose eyes tell you he hates the world and wants to punish everyone in and around it, a man whose on borrowed time and wants to exact revenge before he snuffs it. A man whose heart has been broken and life shattered, a man's whose soul mate left him for no good reason and took his entire world with her as she did. I see a man with nothing left because of a woman, a man whose been chewed up and spat out and wants to make her suffer for it. I see that she is going to die and then he will be free to blow us all up.

I see the end of the world coming and I don't know what to do.

Then out of nowhere everything changes.

# Chapter 46

The following things all happen instantly in the next few seconds.

The delicate, flailing, desperate arm of Phil's dying wife appears from nowhere clutching the detonator behind his back. She flings it in one smooth, quick motion over her head and out of the back of the van.

I follow its trajectory and see it land in the centre of the car park and skid 10 - 15 feet away from the van.

Everything stops.

I gasp, alerting Phil to my presence.

Our eyes meet; Him crouching over his wife trying to strangle her - me lying flat on my stomach on the floor under his van.

I scramble to my feet and sprint wildly for the detonator, springing clumsily from my prostrate position under the doors. Out of the corner of my eye, as I sprint out past the open doors of the van, I can see Phil getting to his feet and reaching for something. I also see Phil's wife tumble out of the van backwards, gasping for breath and clutching at her neck as she collapses to the concrete floor.

I run quickly and cross the ground with ease. I scoop the detonator up with without breaking my gait and start for the nearest exit.

Then I hear a gun cock behind me.

Then I hear a gun explode behind me as I try to make a getaway.

I feel something tear a hole in the back of my right leg and I cry out in agony. I stumble, scream, drop the detonator and fall to my knees.

The detonator slides out in front of me and I hear Phil dismount the van behind, its suspensions protesting heavily as he unloads his overweight frame.

I find some resolve and perseverance from somewhere and drag myself back to my feet. Limping, crying in pain, I hop a few more steps and retrieve the detonator once again.

I try to hop further, my right leg dead and lifeless as I move, and then a gun cocks behind me again. Then I hear a gun fire once more.

I feel a hole tear through my spine, and am thrown several feet across the floor.

I feel the concrete cradle my face and the blood seep from my wounds.

I hear footsteps moving ever closer.

I see the detonator off to my right. It has been thrown across the floor one too many times and is now in several pieces.

I see that it's not fit for purpose anymore.

I see that I might just have stopped this.

I flip onto my back and I see Phil looming over me.

He has his pistol pointed down at me.

I see his shadow cloak me in the gloom of death.

I see joy on his face and I see him smile as he waves his gun at me.

"You should have stayed out of this my friend. YOU SHOULD HAVE FUCKING LEFT ME ALONE!"

Then I close my eyes, because I'm about to die.

## Chapter 47

So I'm momentarily knocked out and wake up with a gun in my mouth. Phil is knelt on my chest - his manic eyes are inches from my face; His overweight frame crushing my lungs and slowly seeping the life from me. Why he hasn't killed me already is anyone's guess, but from the demonic, possessed look on his face suggests he wants to see me suffer first? I may just have foiled his plan and I think he wants to torture me for a bit because of this.

He is snarling words at me that I can barely understand as my ears ringing wildly again, blood running down my right cheek. A liquid also runs down the back of my right leg, and I assume it's from the gunshot wound and not my bladder.

Over his shoulder I see his wife fleeing from the scene. I also see the vans destructive cargo still lying in wait, but now the detonator is off to my right in pieces. Phil eyes the detonator and his fleeing wife and is further enraged - he swings his elbow across the side of my face and screams more things in my face. I can taste all of the following things at this point: blood, sweat, saliva, metal, powder and oil.

'WHY DID YOU HAVE TO GET INVOLVED?' Phil's screaming at

me, whilst taking a couple more swipes with his elbow; Each one giving me a brief window for breath as he has to remove the gun from my mouth to do so. Each one chipping a tooth or two as he shoves the barrel back down my throat.

  I swallow several chunks of enamel during these blows. The barrel of the gun tastes smooth and polished against my tongue and I can feel tiny indentations and markings along the surface with it.

  I came to be a hero, to do something, to make a difference, to make an impact - and I know I have, but it will have cost me my life. I am strangely content knowing this as I try to decipher the guns markings with my tongue. The bile and rage spewing forth from my attacker is irrelevant at this point.

  I know all these things at this point; this will be my last day on earth, I saved hundreds of lives; Alice will be safe; I have achieved something in my life at last; it is hard to breath with a gun in your mouth; having a 15 stone man pressing on your chest is uncomfortable; Alice will take care of Dex for me; and that I will make the news.

  Phil pulls the gun out of my mouth, his tears shower my face, and he strikes me across the side of the head with the butt of the pistol. I black out again and must be seconds from death because various things flash before my eyes.

I see myself wetting the bed as a kid, calling for a mother who doesn't appear. I see my dad drinking heavily on my birthday whilst my mother lambastes him for it. Later I see dad disappear forever after he and mum had a huge row. I see myself running away from home as a teenager and sleeping on various friends' floors. Eventually returning to the family home later, just in time to watch my mother get ill and die in front of me months later. I see myself losing my virginity to a hooker at 17 - spending £60 for the pleasure. I see flashes of my various careers including roadie, musician, writer, magician, window cleaner, electrician, painter and decorator and psychic. I see Dex licking my face to wake me up from a hideous hangover and Alice snuggling up to me in the back of the cinema. I see my shitty flat complete with rising damp and various stains. I see myself sleeping rough in the back of my trailer.

I think of the time I took Alice to the local pub for a Sunday carvery and she spilt cranberry sauce all over the floor, enraging the manager and causing a spat between us, which ultimately left us out on the street hungry. I remember when she told me that the quickest way to a woman's heart is too make her laugh and that my barrage of lame joke's seemed to do the trick. There was the trip to the Zoo we took together, where we taunted the chimps with bananas and I pretended not too be scared by the tarantulas.

   Here on the floor, already seriously wounded and seconds from a final fatal shot, all I can think of is her and how my life has been infinitely illuminated by her simply being in it. Here on my grey death bed my life has boiled down to her and it's all I need.

   I think I'm smiling, but I can't tell because of the pistol. I see the future and I see her in it. I see her having a long and prosperous life, making a full recovery and moving to London to pursue her dreams. I see her taking care of Dex in a modest but plentiful studio flat. There are designs, machines and fabric off-cuts all around as she starts her journey into the cut throat world of fashion.

   I see that this has been worthwhile after all and that my life has not been for nothing.

   I feel pride.

   I feel security.

   I feel content.

I feel resolution.

I see Alice happy and it's all I need.

I see her smile and I am ready for death.

I close my eyes because I'm ready for death.

I hear a gunshot and am ready for death.

## Chapter 48

I wake up later.

I'm staring up at a plain white ceiling. I am being rushed quickly down a hallway as the fluorescent tube lights flash by above.

I cannot move a muscle and have tubes sticking out of my arm and a mask on my face. This mask is attached to a large balloon that some young lad is squeezing intermittently to fill my lungs with air.

There are several other people around me as I lay helpless on the gurney. These people are all dressing in the same blue clothing.

I am to assume I'm in a hospital. This scares me because I hate hospitals.

I see this guy helping me breath scream something to his friends, and instantly someone else appears with a different mask. This gets placed over my mouth and nose and my head fills with a strange gas.

I pass out.


It's later now, and I'm in a bed alone. From my vantage

point, I can see only machines, tubes, dials, bedding, and ceiling tiles. I am drowsy, intoxicated and scared. Various machines surround me and look to be keeping me alive - right now I think this might be Heaven, but it could just as easily be in Hell.

   I spend a while drifting in and out of consciousness for a period of time, I can't establish. I also struggle to establish whether I'm alive, dead or in some kind of cruel limbo? Each time I briefly open my eyes I see various things. These include a cast of nurses carrying out various procedures that include blood test, tube replacement, machine monitoring, personal cleaning and temperature taking. Once I see a serious looking Doctor with a clipboard and a stern look on his face, he was reading some dials above my head - he wasn't happy with them. There was a turbulent time when I woke up convulsing and with a cast of frenetic people around me - one of whom shoved a needle in my arm and I fell asleep again.

   I woke up briefly one time and saw Alice at my bed side. I tried to scream, I tried to talk, and I tried to move. Nothing! Each time I woke, I wasn't able to make any contact with the people round me. All I could see were concerned faces and machines. All I could hear where beeps, screams and deafening silence.

All I could feel was dead.

I didn't die in the parking lot, but I didn't leave alive either.

I left in limbo. I left in a coma.

I slept for days, weeks, months, years? I was alive and dead at the same time.

I was Schrödinger's cat.

I was a burden.

I was a living, breathing, machine hybrid.

AC power was my oxygen; machines were my saviours and captors all at once. Without them I would have died back on that concrete floor, without them life can't survive such bullet wounds.

For a while I existed on the edge of life; Skirting dangerously from death to life, life to death, from breathing naturally to being forced to breathe by an appliance. At times I wished I was dead and that Phil finished me properly.

For a while I was being stalked around a vacant shopping mall by Phil's ghost. All around I could see the destruction and rubble of Phil's intentions, of Phil's successful plan. I see the death and destruction, the blood and the bodies, the hell on earth. I step in, over and around, debris and body parts, as a spectre lingers in the distance behind me. This is the spectre of Phil and he has a bullet wound in his forehead. He is pointing in my direction and mouthing words that I cannot make out, his pale face a vision of calm and stillness as he holds up a bloody forefinger, this forefinger points past me into the distance. I follow its trail and look up at the giant ornate Christmas tree behind me in the centre of the mall. It is a picture of festive beauty, perfectly untouched and pristine in amongst the wreckage and carnage wrought by Phil's bomb.

Alice's corpse sits on top of it where the angel should be.

I collapse to my knees and let out a silent scream, as Alice's bloodied crucified corpse suddenly springs to life - her dead white eyes gazing down at me.

"Why didn't you save me Billy…" her corpse greets.

"Why didn't you save me…?"

"Why didn't you save me…?"

"Why didn't you save me…?" It pleads, as my mind

disintegrates.

For a while nothing existed for me and for large chunks of time my mind didn't exist either.

For a while dreams like these were all that I knew.

Blackness consumed me - terror was all I knew.

Then one day, I finally woke up.

# Chapter 49

I see Alice as I wake.

She is at my bedside sleeping peacefully. I gaze at her as she sits slumped in an armchair at the side of my bed, seemingly dreaming contently. She is dressed in casual jogging bottoms and a hoodie, and wearing a beanie hat that shrouds her beautiful hair, hair that normally frames her face perfectly.

I assume it must be cold outside and in the midst of winter, but my mind is so groggy and confused, I struggle to make any sense of anything regarding seasons or weather. My senses are raw and shocked by the stimuli in the room. I lie encased in a hospital bed that is tilted at a 30 degree angle to raise my torso and head slightly. Surrounding the head of my bed are the various machines that are still keeping me alive, still making all manner of noises, as I gaze around at them. Off too my right is a drip that's terminating in my right arm, burrowed deep into a vein, and I can feel the liquid pulsing through it a I poke at my exposed arm. This foreign liquid, this stuff seems to be keeping me alive still, and it is a terrifying sight.

I breathe slowly and try to gather my thoughts, trying to stave of the panic and the terror, trying to be grateful that I seemingly survived. The room is peaceful and still aside from the tick of the machines and the deep breathing of Alice as she sleeps.

I ponder how long she has been at my side, as a whole table of flowers and gifts off to my left are showing visible signs of decay. This table has piles of fruit and bouquets of flowers, which are long overdue disposal. I can see fading peaches, blackened bananas and wilting roses - I can see death around me in fruit and fauna form. I ponder that I may have been neglected, given up on, or abandoned as a patient given the decay in the room - I may have been a lost cause?

There are also rows and rows of cards on this table. A lot of them say 'THANK YOU' in varying shapes and sizes, colours and styles. A few say 'HERO,' and I ponder where you could purchase such a card? I guess that they must be handmade, or custom online cards and this makes me feel even more special. I think I did good.

I think I survived, but I can't be too sure because this all looks too much like some version of heaven. Alice at my side, adulation and congratulations from strangers, private wards, seemingly surviving multiple gunshot wounds? This all feels too much.

I gaze deeply at Alice and watch her chest rise and fall as she sleeps, huddled up in the small arm in the corner. She looks serene and peaceful, she looks content and at ease. I am stunned and surprised that she is here, and I guess I must be the luckiest man in the world, because I thought I'd never see anyone again, let alone the love of my life.

I look closer at her concealed hairline, thinking it's strange to see her in such a hat, as I've never known her to wear such a thing in all the years we've known each other. I see bald, stubble patches sneaking out from below the rim of the beanie hat, I see a lack of eyebrows on her face, and I see the pale, skinny frame of a cancer patient.

Now this all feels like some version of hell.

Alice has cancer, I seem to have been in some kind of induced sleep/coma, I may have compromised use of my body if I ever leave here, various machines are keeping me alive, and fruit is rotting in the corner. This must be hell - this must be purgatory.

Then Alice's eyes flutter open and she looks at me from

across the room. My heart skips a beat and a smile spreads so wide across her face that it makes me feel like this could be the greatest moment of my life.

She slowly composes herself and silently, with care, approaches my bedside. She cradles my face with her frail, cold hands, and kisses me on the forehead. A kiss that is dry, compassionate, loving and thankful, a kiss that tells me I've done good and that she is happy to see me awake.

"My Hero," she says softly as she gazes deep into my groggy soul.

Right now she is looking at me like it actually means something to her that I survived.

Right now, I'm back in Heaven.

# Chapter 50

So I try to speak to her as she sits at my bedside cradling my hands in hers. She is visibly excited to see me alive and kicking, so surprised in fact that I wonder if I was every supposed to wake up from this? So surprised that I'm even conscious, and that I must have been pretty far from living for quite some time.

I try to speak, but now realise I can't because there is a tube sticking out the side of my mouth. It runs to another machine at my bedside and is providing some function that I assume is also necessary to keep me alive? Anyway it prescience, crawling down into my throat, stops me from verbalising any actual words to Alice as she gazes up at me.

"Hey, Hey, No, Don't play with any of this stuff, its important stupid," she interjects softly, as I fumbles at the pipes invading my mouth.

I am desperate to speak, desperate to tell Alice I love her, desperate to get some breakdown of events, desperate to not feel scared anymore. The last thing I can remember is a madman jamming a pistol in my mouth and now I'm awake in a hospital, surrounded by machines and a loved one who's clearly been through the ringer herself. She looks meek, tired and ill, and I know Dex was right and that the big C has come for her - I want to save her again and I want to not be breathing through a tube. I want to get out of this bed and see my best friend, I want to taste something other than blood, I want to be a living human being again rather than an organism attached to various machines, I want to get back to my shitty little flat.

Emotion overwhelms me and tears start to flow as nurse rushes in and start fiddling with some of the machines around me, machines that have started making loud noises all of a sudden. These noises could be good or bad, I'm not sure.

Panic replaces calm and the claustrophobia of this bed is overwhelming. A machine off to my left starts buzzing and beeping faster as my heart rate starts to rise. I try to raise a hand, but Alice catches it. I try to move but am entombed by various casts and several layers of blankets. I try to move my legs, but I can't feel them anymore.

Right now I feel paralysed. Right now I feel like this bed is my coffin and the nightmare never actually dissipated, this is just a living version of them.

The tears start to stream as a serious looking doctor

arrives in the room and says some words to the concerned looking nurse at my side. I am scared, because strangers currently know more about my health situation than I do. I look at Alice like I might be dying again, but she just looks up at me with a serene calm that isn't in fitting with the scene.

"It's ok, it's ok..." Alice softly consoles, kissing my prostrate right hand as she cradles its,

"Calm down, you're ok now. Everything's ok now. These are good noises," she continues, and despite all the drama and panic around, and the ever louder beeping machines - I start to think I might be alright in the end.

It's later now and everything has settled down.

For a while this room was a parade of doctors, surgeons, physicians, nurses, cleaners and people in posh suits. For a while this room seemed like the only room in world, and for a while there were crowds of people at the door. All craning their necks and jostling for position - all trying to get a sight of me! I'd finally awaken. I was the good news on the ward for a while.

Then everything calmed down again and everyone returned to

whatever they were doing before I woke up. My 15 minutes of fame had ended and someone else's life had to be saved.

Alice never let go of my hand during all of this and when it was quiet, when it was calm, when the world had left my room - she began to talk.

She said a lot of things and she talked until the night came, all the while I was unable to respond, all the while my numerous questions went unheard and unanswered.

These are most of the things she said to me.

She said that I had saved everyone. I had stopped the explosion and the only victims were the two security guards. Phil's 2 tonne fertiliser bomb was disarmed and dismantled safely by experts, no further casualties - I had saved Christmas.

She also told me that a S.W.A.T team had arrived in the parking lot to find Phil about to execute me; they shot on sight and killed him instantly. A stray bullet also hit me in the side of the chest and I was rushed from the scene.

I have been in intensive care since then. I have been in an induced coma since then. I have survived three gunshot wounds.

They were desperate to save me because my other wounds paled in comparison to the one left by their rifles. The on that pierced my lung, the one that required me to have several hours of reconstructive surgery.

She told me that the world has gone mad since then, I have become some kind of saint, some kind of national treasure. She told me that both the Queen and the Prime Minister have been on TV talking about me - The Queen even gave me a special thank you in her Christmas speech! I had saved hundreds of lives by selflessly laying my own on the line.

She has read countless articles about me, she has been constantly harassed by reports, and she has also said a lot of nice things about me too. There have been a lot of debates on many channels about all this, the manufacturing of fertiliser may be changed to make it less explosive thanks to all of this, and regulations may be tightened on pistols.

I might just have changed the world she says.

She has a scrapbook with all this in to show me once I get better, which is good because I can barely believe it.

She tells me Phil's wife made it to safety and has been to visit a few times whilst I've been sleeping, and that she is leading a campaign for me to get some kind of medal of honour, OBE, CBE type of thing. She says Phil's wife has apologised for all of this, and that she is racked with quilt over her betrayal of what was once a good, kind, man. She feels responsible in some kind of way, which I guess she is on some level, but she hasn't got three gunshot wounds to show for it - just the one - so I struggle to feel too sorry for her.

Alice says that when I get better there is a pile of cheque's waiting for me. They are donations from the people I saved, they are 'Thank You' cards from most of the people at the mall that day, and there is a lot of charity and goodwill towards me.

There is also a undercurrent of scepticism. People are confused as to how I knew what I knew. Alice has been questioned several times by the police, she was a suspect and potential accomplish for a while. Some people need this explaining and just saying I can see the future doesn't seem to cut it. Some people still think I was in on this until the very last minute, and that I was an accomplice who had a sudden change of heart.

Alice's timeline, explanations, and evidence of our activities, have dispelled doubt for the authorities - but the world is still sceptical. To some I'm a suspicious figure and to the rest - well, this is all something they will never really want to understand.

People just can't see the future they say. Real heroes don't exist they say. There's a lot more going on behind the scenes, there's a suspicious side to all of this to some people.

Alice tells me that she has had Dex with her ever since and that he misses me. She says that somehow, he knows I'm ok and that I'm coming home one day, and that he waits by the caravan door every day for me to come home.  That he was found safe and sound at the camp site and she took him in whilst all this played out. She tells me she and her brothers are camping in the area, and they are caring for Dex whilst she is having treatment. She's tells me her brothers like me now and that they sent me a card with a small donation in! I saved them and their little sisters lives, and they are forever in my debt, she tells me.

She's also tells me that she found a lump in her breast a while back, and she has been undergoing intensive treatment ever since. She tells me that her connection to me has allowed her fast tracked treatment, the best in the country, and that in the months I've been under, she's been making a good recovery.

She tells me that she knows I already know all this. She tells me that she believes me now, she knows about my gift and she is sorry she ever doubted me. She tells me that this has been a life changing experience for her and that she is eternally grateful for the time we spent together. She says that we are on separate paths now, but that she owes her life to me.

Emotions were high for a while, as she apologies profusely for the way she had treated me and the way that she had left me back there, on that campsite, all those months ago. She said that she wished we could be together, but this is all too much for her now, she is young and ambitious, and that once she is fully recovered, she is off to study fashion. She is off to pursue her dreams.

She said in some papers she had been painted as a harlot who broke the heart of a national treasure, a hussy who is leaving the man that saved her. She said a lot of people still look at her with disdain because of all these gritty details that came out after the inquiries. A lot of people don't want to hear two sides of a story she tells me, through streams of tears - she just wants to disappear sometime soon, she says.

There is a book deal and film deal in the offing once I make a full recovery - I am to be forever famous for this she tells me.

Everything changed on Christmas Eve for everyone - the world focused its attention on me on Christmas Eve and I've been asleep the whole time she says.

Alice says a lot to me that I can't take in or process properly. There are just too many strands of life changing information to take in all at once - A man waking from a coma cannot process such information properly.

All I know is that I'm alive and will survive all this. So is Alice, so is Dex. That's all that really matters right now.

Oh she also told me the shot in the back has paralysed me, and I will never walk again - but I can't really deal with that right now.

# Chapter 51

How they rip you off at the fair part 5 - Test your strength.

Otherwise known as - how big is your dick? The most chauvinistic, macho, outdated game you'll ever see this one. Hit a pad very hard with a giant mallet and a puck will shoot up the tower, hit said pad hard enough and the puck will strike a bell at the top of the tower and you will win something.

Back in the early days of the fair this was the most rigged, tampered with, and impossible game you could choose - it was also the one that the carnie would exploit people with the most. See the game used to be heavily controlled, the carnie would have complete command over whether the bell would ring or not - regardless of a players strength or technique. As you can imagine, he would use this to exploit as much cash and entertainment as possible from onlookers and passers-by.

It would play out like this:

The cheeky guy would pick out the smallest, weediest guy

he could see passing and, using his charm and wit, get him to have a go at ringing the bell. He would control the game so that this tiny man would ring the bell on his first attempt.

Cue all the big guys stepping forward to prove their worth. Cue the carnie rigging the game so that they would fail repeatedly. Much humiliation and damaged male pride would follow, as the alpha males were ridiculed and teased by the gathered crowd and carnie showman for their numerous failed attempts.

Many repeated attempts later, the carnie would finally let these embarrassed muscle men win the game and then the next guy would step up, thus the cycle would continue. A skilled carnie could whip up quite the show with a carefully rigged machine and the right mix of spectators and competitors. All based on the male compulsion to prove strength and show off of course, all based on men wanting to compare the size's of their dicks.

Such control of the apparatus was possible because back in the early days these machines were handmade with a combination of wood, nails and levers. The Puck was attached to a taught cable that ran up the tower to the bell; the puck could slide up and down this cable easily if permitted. The game would be rigged to allow the carnie to step on an indistinguishable plank in the floor that would slacken this cable. The result would be a cable so loose and slack, that no matter how hard the hammer was struck, pure friction would prevent it from ever reaching the bell.

You can imagine the fun that would be had taunting the most muscular men at the fair and watching in pure amusement, as a young child would be allowed to strike the bell with ease after their testosterone fuelled failures.

These days of course the machines are spring loaded and not remotely rigged in such a way. Today they are fibreglass, plastic monstrosities with numerous glaring lights and even digital displays. It still attracts the same type of macho showboating, but it's not controlled by the carnie anymore as the machines aren't handmade - thus there not really much fun anymore. If you do stumble across an old fashioned hand-made version make sure to avoid it, because it's just there to humiliate you.

There is still a knack to winning though and that is accuracy not strength. Most people swing wildly with the oversized mallet and strike the pad off centre and without any accuracy - such an uncontrolled swing isn't conducive to a good strike.

You have to aim for the dead centre of the pad. Holding the mallet as far down the shaft as possible whilst still achieving a firm grip. Placing both hands right near the end of the shaft, so you can achieve maximum arch when you swing. You have to practice this full arched swing a few times before going for it, swinging the mallet through its full arch to accustom yourself with its weight and feel, like a golfer preparing for a shot with a few practice swings. Only once your happy with you aim and have perfected your swing should you put you full force behind it.

It can be beaten easily this one but it used to be nigh on impossible. It used to be primarily used to ridicule and embarrass all those muscle men that strut around. It used to be the highlight of the fair.

## Chapter 52

A long time has passed since the hospital - since Christmas Eve. It's a year or so after I left in a wheelchair and I'm back at the day job now, back in the caravan. The great Psy Paxley has made his comeback.

A lot changed in the months after I left the hospital. In fact everything changed, and it's with a yearning for normality, and a touch of nostalgia, that I've returned to the old fortune teller grind. It's not quite the same old grind it used to be though - this time I'm on tour. This time I'm popping up all around the country in city centres with my van and my dog. People queue for hours to see me. It's not the same job I've been doing for decades, but its close enough to feel comfortable.

See I'm a star now.

I spent months in and out of papers, magazines, talk shows, websites, news reels etc. You name it; I've been on in or in it. It's been bizarre, but I guess when the world finds out someone can see the future - they all want a piece. I've signed a book deal, there will be a film with a glamorous movie star portraying me, I've made a lot of money.

Now I'm bored with all that and I just want to get back in my van with my dog and read the fortunes of random strangers again. I wanted to return to the fair and set up in the corner like I always used too, but various people in suits told me that was unrealistic now. Apparently I can't just be normal now. Either that, or there was so much money in doing a tour like this, that they had to make it happen.

See everyone lies to me now and treats me like a commodity, so I never know what to believe. I just did what I though was right and now I need a manager, agent, lawyer and consultant - just to do what I did for the majority of my life.

Also the gypsy van I spent years in has been modified, upgraded and expanded, to accommodate my wheelchair. I never walked out of that hospital after all. I haven't walked since the day at the mall. Phil left his mark on me and it's something I've had to have a lot of counselling to come to terms with. Who needs legs anyway right? It was a brutal, harsh price to pay, and one that has taken me some time to come to terms with. I have been seeing a shrink for some time and throwing myself into other things as a distraction - I'm now studying art and learning to paint. I also have an autobiography to finish.

Other things that have changed include a cured Alice leaving for London to study fashion.

She said she loved me, and then left forever.

She said one day we will be together - but that isn't now.

Me and Dex now live in a swanky middleclass detached house. He has a girlfriend called Debra. Debra is a guide dog of sorts, whose been expertly trained to aid me during my daily activities. She now fetches me stuff that I can't be bothered to fetch, and generally makes me feel dumb and useless. Still, Dex loves her, and they run around the large garden endlessly as I watch peacefully from the window.

For a while everything happened that could possibly be deceived - then for a while after nothing happened. After the hysteria and the buzz, after the 15 minutes, the world looked elsewhere and life settled down again.

Suddenly I was living the middles class lifestyle that Phil was. Suddenly I was dull, wheelchair bound, and jobless. So I got back on the road, and now there is another young lady sat opposite me in my van, waiting for a miracle, expecting a life changing experience.

Now everyone expects me to change their lives.

So I ask for this young things watch and she hands it over expectantly, a look of awe and inspiration in her eyes as she does so. She is an attractive young brunette, late teens, with a youthful complexion and optimism that reminds me of Alice. From the excitement on her face I'm guessing she's only here because she wants to tell everyone on social media that she met a celeb. She'll take a selfie with me at some point I'm guessing.

These are the type clientele I deal with nowadays. Young people who are enticed by the fame and celebrity status I seem to hold, people with enough spare time to stand in a long queue on a Saturday. Now I'm just 'that guy in the paper', and meeting me makes a great social network status update. Now, because I'm 'the man who can see the future', I only get people coming along who have nice comfortable lives and no real issues or problems. I don't see a lot of pain or despair anymore because people avoid me if there on troubled paths, or wrestling with big decisions. It seems a lot of people cant handle the truth, or are afraid or it - so I just get happy go lucky types who want to know about exam results, or there chosen career paths.

Also I no longer bother with any dice, cards, or props. A lot of the theatre is gone from my act because people don't need convincing anymore. Now people hang on my every word and just believe everything I say - no more convincing or acting. So I clutch the skinny leather watch and focus. The young lady gasping in awe as I do this, *OMG Right!!!*

I see a young girl who is popular and sociable, having the time of her life as she finishes college. She's studying health and beauty and is obsessed with preening and fashion - surrounded by similar young ladies, whose lives revolve around looking good and staying thin.

She is young, naïve and full of zest. She's enthusiastic about leaving home, about studying Make up and Beauty at a university the other end of the country. She too is following her dream, and wants to work with the stars and models on fashion shoots and film sets; she wants the glamour and the glitz.

I see her shedding tears as her mum and dad drop her off at her new dorm and leave her to fend for herself for the first time in her life. She is scared, alone, and not too fond of her new roommate - a butch and stocky lesbian studying sports therapy.

   This new life is tough for her and many a night she cries herself to sleep as she misses her group of girls, her mother's home cooked meals, her dads comforting shoulder. She is growing up fast and coming to terms with life slowly.

   I see boys come and go as the party hard, you only live once, lifestyle of university hits her hard. She's still crushingly naïve and gets used and abused by several guys, all of whom didn't have to struggle too hard to talk their way into her pants.

   I see her become good friends with her surely roommate - she's just so different from all her old friends - and I see this new friend comfort her after every one night stand. After every playboy never calls her back after getting what he wanted.

   Our girl struggles through the first year, but returns for the second year with a renew vigour and optimism. She can do this and she is starting to grow up fast she thinks. The time at home with her parents over, the holidays was stifling and controlling, and our young babe just wants to be independent now.

   I see her get drunk, take some pills, smoke some weed, and

snort a line. I see visions of our young, innocent young lady, dissolving into a wild and hard partying woman. Suddenly she starts to attract a lot of friends, a lot of attention, and a lot of men. She now starts to use and abuse them instead.

Until I see her party that little too hard with a couple of guys she doesn't really know. I see her get heavily intoxicated and partake in a semi-consensual threesome with these partial strangers. I see the shame on her face the next morning and the vomit as she realises just how low she sank.

Flash to a few months later and she's taking medication for Chlamydia and trying to recover from the psychological torment of an early abortion. See she never saw those guys again and certainly didn't want a child at such a young age. Flash to a typically distraught night where our girl is in tears and being comforted by her butch roommate. She is being told how terrible men are and how she should avoid them because they're just after one thing.

The next morning these roommates wake up in the same bed, virtually naked, and our girl has been seduced into her first lesbian experience.

Flash through awkward conversations, more tears, more

recriminations, and more angst. Later, she moves back home to her parents, abandoning her studies. She can't stand to be around there anymore because everyone knows about her mistakes and her transgressions.

She can't stay there anymore because her roommate fell in love with her that night, but our girl is only full of regret and shame. I see her mum and dad giving her a stern talking too and chastising her for ruining her future. I see the shame on their faces that the studying and debt will all be for nothing. For a while everything falls apart.

Then I see her a decade later. She's all grown up and living with another women. That one night did eventually change everything for her, she is now happily engaged to a loving woman. They have a lovely small house and our girl has a small chain of hair and beauty salons.

She finally made it. She's not living her original dream, but a good enough version of it. She grew up a lot in those intervening years. She learned a lot of life lessons that eventually paid off.

I see all this and then I tell her to be herself - to follow her dreams and embrace uncertainty. I tell her that she will party hard, study hard, have fun, shed tears and eventually live a happy and fulfilled life. I tell her that a lot of adventure, experimentation and regret are coming her way, and that she should just embrace it because in the end it all works out.

In the end it always works out, I say.

Life is too be lived so enjoy the ride I saw, life is a wild, roller coaster so hang on tight I say, the future changes us all I say, and you won't be the same person you are now in a decade or two I say.

See, I never used to think people wanted to know the gritty details of their future, but now they expect it from me. I tell them everything I see and I tell them that fate is in their hands now.

See, I can see the future and I will tell it to these people now. I want to tell them now, because I'm living proof that you can take your future into your own hands and shape it, and mould it, to your will.

The future isn't set in stone, so I tell her everything I've seen, and I also tell her it's all in her hands now.

I used to think people didn't really want to know what the future had in store for them; I used to think it was too bleak and uninspiring to please them. Now I know that it's liberating - its life changing.

I can see the future - and now you can change it.

Right now I look like a completely different person to the one I used to be.

Printed in Great Britain
by Amazon.co.uk, Ltd.,
Marston Gate.